WHITE LIES

Dexter Petley lives in a caravan in the Burgundy mountains, writing, fishing and gardening. He has published two previous novels, *Little Nineveh* and *Joyride*. He is also a regular contributor to *Waterlog, The Magazine for the Absolute Angler*.

For more information on Dexter Petley, visit www.4thestate.com/dexterpetley

WHITE LIES

Dexter Petley

FOURTH ESTATE • *London* and *New York*

This paperback edition first published in 2004
First published in Great Britain in 2003 by
Fourth Estate
A Division of HarperCollins*Publishers*
77–85 Fulham Palace Road
London W6 8JB
www.4thestate.com

1 3 5 7 9 8 6 4 2

A catalogue record for this book is available from the
British Library.

ISBN 0–00–729228–7

Typeset by Rowland Phototypesetting Limited,
Bury St Edmunds, Suffolk.
Printed in Great Britain by
Clays Ltd, St Ives plc

FOR LAURE

PART 1

ONE

We were in a supermarket in Flers that Saturday afternoon last January. Joy was choosing things you wouldn't buy if you were planning to leave your husband, unless she was stocking up for the unexpected, the bare cupboard I didn't know was coming. But there was something wrong, she was low-speed, and anything I said echoed and died out like a weighted sack of words dropped into a winter pond.

I saw her clutch a bag of flour like she couldn't let it go, her bottom lip pegged in her teeth. Did I catch her in the act of planning or had she just made the decision, and was wondering if she really wanted to leave me with a bag of flour I wouldn't need? I must've tipped the balance, if there was still a balance, when I said: *what d'you want that for?*

If she stood here now I wouldn't say: when did you decide to leave me, which item in the trolley was the last moment of our marriage? She'd picked a tin of chickpeas instead of dry ones, holding her breath like she was weighing up the future.

— We can't afford these bloody tins, I said, snatching it off her and clunking it back on the shelf, jumping back in time and trying to change events. She'd run out of last straws right then.

We drove home through mist like a stocking

over your head, down lanes invisible under tractor mud. The Land Rover cab was cold and streaming, the glaze channels on the door-tops completely rusted away, the windows held in place with splints of oak lathe from our ceiling. I said: *what are you so fucking miserable about?* Shouted it really, because we had to shout to hear ourselves above the roar of the diesel engine.

— I need some time to myself, she'd shouted back. I have to go away, to be alone.

I spent the rest of the weekend in a dumb panic. She'd ask me to wait outside while she made phone calls, and once there I began to map out my future alone. I occupied myself with the twenty-year-old hay-bales, dragging them out the barns and up the back garden, cutting the hemp string, the bales springing open like accordions into cakes. I mulched the vegetable beds, one square hay cake at a time, but they were too compact so I pulled them all apart and scattered them loose and thick. Then Joy banged on the window and I stood there as she handed me a cup of tea. She made small talk and offered me a home-made biscuit like she was the widow of the place, old Madame Macé, and I was the silent, respectful gardener.

— I'll only be gone a week, she said, coming outside and standing on the well cover. The dark green box hedge behind her, the sound of a man we'd never seen calling his dog.

— You're not coming back, I said, I know you're not coming back.

— I'm your friend, she said, but the hug was all jacket and mittens, her body already gone. I don't have anything to give you right now . . .

I didn't dare ask what she meant. I didn't even ask who she'd phoned or where she was going. I stretched every minute till it snapped and blanked out the whole of the coming week. She said she'd booked a ticket on the Eurostar shuttle, and she asked me if I'd drive her to the station Monday morning, like she was a guest who wanted to get the train to Paris.

This was the first time she'd left anyone, perhaps the first time she'd ever lied, so she hadn't known that all deserters say: *I just need time to think, it's not you, I'm your friend, don't worry.* I'd done it before almost word for word, amazed at how easy it was to get away with. It was no different now, only I was the shocked one, willing to agree to anything, but not wanting to know what I'd done wrong. *When I get back we'll talk*, she said. I remained grateful for every kind word, but we knew there'd be no talk.

She was my executioner, quick, tidy, purposeful, letting me spend my last hours outside where, by Sunday, I was just hanging about, gripping on to corner-stones or gutterpipe, crying against the seized-up baler rusting down by the *mare*. I'd kick its solid rubber wheels, homing on their details to alleviate the distress. I noticed they'd come off a British Army gun carriage made in Birmingham in 1942. I tried to concentrate on the effects of this war and forget Joy, but I couldn't eat and she had to sit on my lap to help me drink the tea. So I felt like a war veteran too, trembling on a stick on a last visit to France, to this farm where the battle took place in the German retreat. We were surrounded by souvenirs of that battle and the occupation. A German Officer's pocket inkwell Joy had found just by putting her hand under the cider press. Track-wheels off Panzer tanks stuck upright in the garden for periwinkles to climb. US Army jerrycans, 1943, on the Land Rover roof rack. A German-French dictionary, Berlin 1941. Hitler Pfennigs and machine-gun bullets lying unused in their hundreds on the floor in rotten layers of grain and in the recesses of every barn wall. There were live shells still on a window ledge and the aluminium box we'd scuffed out from under the chicken house with the words *US Army Bomb Mechanism* on it. Water canteens and leather webbing and big brass shell cases with greasy rags tied over the top which old Farmer Macé had used as rust-proof paint pots. And the mound of heavy leather army horse tack from the beginning of the war.

Our conversation evaded concrete futures. Joy listed the small things I could get on with while she was away. I swallowed the lies like they were pep pills. If I strayed into emotive areas she'd say *don't*, so I didn't. I shut off my mind so the imaginary time between her leaving and her coming back would cease to exist beyond that domestic span of going up the field to check on the goats or gathering wood for the night.

*   *   *

On Sunday morning Joy wove a band of lavender for my fishing hat then asked me to stay outside till she banged on the window with a mug of tea. I went chopping wood, smashing up old oak planks, so worm-eaten they were half powder. Monsieur Aunay's grandson came by on the Mobylette to check on some beasts in the top field. I'd only ever seen him at apple gathering, in the back of the cart with the whole family. Now he looked like he was on a rite of passage, his first solo task. He'd borrowed his *grandpère*'s Mobylette and white crash helmet and he wore a new pair of blue overalls. He checked the *bœuf* and pushed the Mobylette homeward down the muddy track. I swung the axe a few more times but there he was, standing beside me, holding out a piece of paper. Fund-raising to renovate the *salle des fêtes* at Landigou, ten francs a scratch card. I bought one, he stood there as I scratched it. *Vous avez perdu.*

On Monday morning I could see Joy was holding her breath, crossing her fingers, suppressing that rising triumph of getting away, or the terror in case the Land Rover wouldn't start or the train was cancelled. I played my part to perfection too, and if she noticed maybe she was grateful. For me it was not an act of love but contrition, letting her believe she wasn't lying, that she was just taking time out from a lifelong commitment and in the process helping herself over a period of self-doubt.

There wasn't time, and it wasn't Joy sitting there now. In this woman's haste to get away from me, the future image of herself had slipped its lead and pulled ahead, choking and laughing. Just simple but significant changes, like she didn't drink coffee that morning. *It makes me manic*, she said, like it'd been a lifelong tendency and she was talking to an acquaintance years hence.

As we got in the Land Rover she said to the geese: *bye you lot* and I knew my last chance had gone. It was the farewell I never got.

Monday was market day in Briouze. We followed our neighbours' tractors with their orange beacons flashing in the mist, the breath of lumbering beasts billowing through the slats of *vacheres* towed by mud-lagged Land Cruisers and crapped-on Renault vans. It was the perfect time to turn her back on the place.

We stood on the railway platform away from the smokers. She acted like we were strangers, stepping on a train to be a single girl travelling alone in France, with no winter clothes in her rucksack. I didn't know she'd packed the silk shirts and cotton socks, the brown dress and safari shorts. Or that she'd be back in Africa before I could sleep again.

The train came in like a row of linked tombs. I tried to say something but my mouth was cold, I couldn't feel my lips and my jaw locked shut.

— Buck-up, she said.

She gave me her cheek as I went to kiss her mouth, and I caught her smell for a keepsake. By the end of the week it would disappear from her clothes and the bed as the mould and damp remains of Le Haut Bois took over.

She'd once called me 'the unlucky explorer' from
some poem it doesn't matter who wrote:

> *And all my endeavours are unlucky explorers*
> *come back, abandoning the expedition;*
> *the specimens, the lilies of ambition*
> *still spring in their climate, still unpicked;*
> *but time, time is all I lacked*
> *to find them, as the great collectors before me.*

TWO

I'd read about *Joy The Gold-Panning Missionary* long before I met her. A flowery article beside an inky newsprint photo in *Viva*, a Nairobi women's magazine which Zanna showed me.

Zanna was twenty years older than me. We met in London at a Somali literacy gig in Whitechapel. She was thin, with blue tracing-paper skin, dressed in black with a beehive sitting on her head. She kept her money down her bra in a leather pouch and put belladonna drops in her eyes to make them blue. She said her husband Austen lived in Kenya.

She took me back to her flat in Stoke Newington to show me her photos of Africa, her Pokot stools, Karamajong finger knives, Turkana beads and Masai blankets, her *kanzus, kikois* and her paintings of Lake Baringo. She changed into a floor-length tie-dyed jellaba and gave me a *kikoi* to wear while she made us fried-egg sandwiches and told me about Austen. She'd met him in Soho in the fifties when he was a young linguist, half-starved and selling poetry pamphlets outside cafes.

Zanna sold hand-made clothes down Portobello Road and modelled for unknown painters or stashed things for spivs and thugs and Jewish booksellers. She had boxes of photographs of half-starved young men in black rollnecks, gathered like poets outside new coffee bars. Everyone was called Johnny and they were all geniuses, all dead too. Drink, suicide, drugs, starvation, Jack the Knife. When Francis Bacon was starving, Zanna would give him ten bob for a painting. She'd scrape the paint off and sell the canvas down Bayswater to slumming toffs.

— No one wanted one with the fuckin paint still on it, darlin.

Then Austen got a job teaching English in Kenya, so Zanna joined him as his 'disguise'. By now the photos were Kodakolor with white borders: Austen turned half native, half Africa bum in his shorts and elephant-hide bush-boots, tea cloth headdress, elder's staff, ten beers a night. In the sixties Austen joined the BBC East Africa Monitoring Unit and they married. He boozed with prostitutes, hunted elephants, camped in lion country and trout fished the Berkshires. The photographs were black and white again: Austen's boot on a dead elephant. Zanna running the camp kitchen. A Sikh mechanic holding a blunderbuss beside the zebra-striped Land Rover.

Soon Austen's prostitutes moved in. Illiterate Kikuyu girls who spent his money on school fees for cousins, seed for their *shambas*, booze, cloth and witch doctors. Zanna painted watercolours and took African lovers, but her life there became a tour of duty whittled down to three months a year, just enough time to extricate Austen from another hoax, disaster or nightmare.

The magazine cutting about Joy was in a box with bundles of aerogrammes hammered into stencils by Austen's typing and his latest photos of dogs, ducks and parched scrub. Austen had come across Joy on one of his walks in Pokotland and suggested *Viva* do an article. Joy, the 29-year-old American missionary helping children pan for gold so they could pay their school fees. Joy, living in a bush village in cattle-raiding country, running the school and a women's self-help group. She rode a motorcycle, wasn't married, and Zanna said she was 'ever so nice' but wasn't really a 'missionary'.

I always told people that my own African past was typical and insignificant. A year in Sudan as a teacher, ten months of it on strike, after which I'd been sacked and drifted along the overland trail of East Africa in my late twenties, trying to find something I could do naturally with little effort, a bit of stringing in Uganda maybe, but always failing to make the breakthrough.

I was thirty then, stuck in London a whole year, incoherent about why I felt drawn back to Africa. Zanna's Africa was a corrupt and dangerous playground which had turned Austen into a reckless adventurer who believed he was indestructible. But he was just a middle-aged man glutting on sex and booze with Kikuyu tarts in native dives.

It was dawn when Zanna suggested we went to bed, even if I wasn't her type. Sex was silent, in the dark made by thick drapes and blankets tacked over the windows. Next day I found the set of clothes Austen kept for his annual week in London. Thornproof suit, impeccable Crombie, shiny brogues. I put them on and wore them for weeks, riding Zanna's black wartime bicycle about town, getting oil on the turnups. I spent her money on an Aeroflot ticket to Nairobi, then thought about what I'd say when I walked into Amolem and asked for Joy.

All Aeroflot flights went to Moscow back in those days. We landed in minus sixteen, got shunted through a terminal behind glass walls and three hundred abandoned boarding gates. Six iron-curtain travellers huddled in the distance with their brown-paper baskets and stringbags. Every gate was blocked by ground staff with guns, boy recruits in military serge, the icy stare of cold raw shaves.

Our passports were taken and replaced by flimsy red cards. We wouldn't be flying on to Nairobi that day and they didn't know when. No plane, bad weather.

The clapped-out airport bus smoked like a burning tyre. It was a mobile coldstore and the driver wore white wellingtons. Hotel reception was like check-in at the morgue. We were all Nairobi bound, all frozen stiff and starting to notice each other for the first time, the pack shuffling into suits. The men had no hand luggage, just the clothes on their backs and the duty-free. The women were mostly mothers with babies, bundles of plastic bags and nappies. The husbands swapped business cards. They all had import/export shops but business was only so-so, which was why we were all flying the cheapest airline in the world.

— This is my Mombasa number . . .

— This is my Bombay address . . .

13

The English lads were bragging.

— Nah, bit of Swahili and they drop at your feet. All you have to say is *hapana mzuri* and you get the lot for nothing . . .

No one edged my way till I was at the desk. It was clear I had to share a room with the bloke behind me.

— I'm Frogget, he said.

— I don't really want to share, I said.

— No trouble. Fuckin shoot through, I will.

He swung a key fob the size of a wooden tennis ball.

— Stops yer puttin it in yer fuckin mouth, dunnit.

He tried it in the lock, upside down. He reeked of Gatwick bars and two-dollar vodkas on the Tupolev over.

— I'll kick the fuckin door in if this key don't fit. It's the way I like to do things, you know, no nonsense, drive it out. That's me. Drive it right out I do.

He threw open the door and swung his plastic bag with the 200 Marlboro on to the first bed and walked straight back out to find the bar. The room was two beds wide, the big triple-glazed window was a glass sandwich and wouldn't close. Net curtains swayed more from heavy filth than wind. Beyond the steps below, there was a perfect surface of untrodden snow. Pine trees lined the road a hundred yards away. Cement trucks and heavy tippers drove by in the dusk which fell like bonfire smoke. The air was pitted with diesel fume and sludge and the airport was lit up by yellow-fever floods. Against the snow a soldier, a gun and a dog.

I fell asleep and woke with a stiff neck from the sub-zero draft to find Frogget rummaging in his carrier bag.

— Run out of fags didn I. Aint you avin tea?

— Where?

— Downstairs, in that canteen.

Frogget tore the wrapping off his box and threw it on the bed, lit one up and left in a puff of smoke. I took the lift downstairs to the canteen and sat on my own in one corner, scratching my dry hair and smoking on a parched throat. A few curled slices of black bread see-sawed on the tablecloth if I touched it. The mothers crowded at the kitchen door for warm baby milk, the men laughed in the bar and the canteen was silent. A Russian waitress brought a plate to my table, picked up the bread, put it on the new plate and brushed crumbs on to the floor.

— Ticket, she said.

— What ticket?

— Meal ticket.

— I haven't got one.

— Reception.

She took the bread away so I walked down the marble stairs to reception. A soldier opened the outer door and snow blew in. He brushed it off his great-coat, stamped his boots and lit up a cigarette. I got the meal ticket and went back to the canteen and the waitress by the tea urn said:

— Sit over there, with your friends.

I joined the only two I recognised from the flight.

— You come for the shit sandwiches? I'm Ray, he's Steve, pleased to meet you.

— Norman, I said.

— How far you going Norman?

— Nairobi.

— What takes you to Kenya then?

— Just a visit, I said. What takes you, Ray?

Frogget came out of the toilet and slammed his beer bottle down, spilling it on his fags and barging in on the conversation.

— Me? he said. You talking about me? I've bin out there a coupla times. Livin on the beaches with them lads that rip off tourists, you know, girls and all. I got a few down there, Malindi, Lamu. You just ask fer me in a bar. Say *mzungu* Frogget and make like you mean I drink a lot. I tell yer, when I'm down there I drink till I don't know where the next one's comin from. Couple o'months an I'll be back 'ome but not before I've whacked it in. Coke, smack, speed, White Cap, Tusker, anything yer like, me. Yeah, smack it up I do.

Ray leaned forward and said:

— You ever chewed that root?

— *Mirrah*, you mean?

— Yeah, that's the stuff. Acid and *mirrah*. Couldn' 'andle that could they, them natives?

Frogget looked at Steve.

— Well Steve, he said. What you up to?

— Yeah Steve, Ray said. What turns you cuckoo?

Steve was still silent, turning a Rothman's packet in his hands, lifting the flap, closing it, putting the packet down. He scratched his leg and sighed before biting his lip.

— Yeah, well, I dunno do I.

— Ah come on Steve, fuck me. You aint goin out there to Kenya to buy a fuckin ice cream, China, I know.

— Well, Steve said, to see what's there I suppose. You know, this and that, here and there.

Ray slapped him on the back and said:

— Well that's about all anyone can do isn't it? That's what I'm going for and I've seen it all before. He'll get a girl. He'll be alright.

I got up and walked off thinking what was so different about me? I was looking for a woman too wasn't I?

Next day the bus took us out to the airport at twenty to midnight, bouncing across the frozen ruts. We were put back in the deserted glass corridors, let loose and ignored. Frogget and Ray were in a bar and Ray was beginning to stagger and sing Polish drinking songs, encouraged by the barmaids with their two-dollar vodkas. Steve was glassy-eyed and wanted to ask me something:

— D'yer reckon I could get to South Africa like, overland?

— Nah, Ray says. No one can. Not even him.

He pointed to an African at the other end of the bar then swayed towards him.

— You won't even get out of Nairobi. *Boukrah.* That's all they ever bleedin say there, *boukrah.* Tomorrow, always bleedin tomorrow. Isn't that right friend?

Ray put his arm round the African's neck and the African pushed it off.

17

— I'm not your friend. I don't even know who you are.

— All Africans are my friends. You're an African, all Africans are my friends, so you're my friend because you need me.

— I don't need you man.

— Yes you do, you need me to look after you. All Africans need me to look after them. I'm the white man and I say *jambo bwana* to the black man. I want you to love me.

He reeled against the wall, bounced off and fell against the African.

— I don't want you to love me, white man. Get your hands off. Don't touch me.

Frogget went over.

— Leave it Ray, you're a public nuisance. You want some village people you should've said, man. Get on down to Lamu.

— No, Ray said, getting a hand on the African's head. Let me kiss you, I want to kiss you, you're my friend.

— Get off. Are you homosexual or something?

The African went to a table and sat down.

— Yeah, alright, I'll be one. I don't mind homosexuals, let me fuck you, come on I want to fuck you.

The African stood and caught Ray by the elbow.

— Fuck off man and leave me alone.

Ray fell against the wall.

— Blacks don't have to like whites any more. You never seen a black man before?

— I'm just having some fun . . .

Ray went along the bar looking for his vodka.

— All these black pigs are the same. He'll get over it.

THREE

One afternoon I found this German helmet while clearing the bank above the *lavoir*. Joy had been gone three days, but when I looked back down the *chemin* at Le Haut Bois nothing told me she'd ever been there. No window steaming as the kettle boiled, no Joy packing logs in the basket, no scubbing of her wellingtons on brittled mud. So I kept away from that house, letting the phone ring and the door clap in a pealing wind. It scraped through the barns day and night and drove sleet-rash into my face, preaching at my chapped lips and fingers.

I'd begun to landscape, starting by the *lavoir* the way me and Joy had meant to, but the earth was frozen shut. Every hamlet in France has a *lavoir*, a water source and washing place. Joy had wanted to turn ours into a water garden, to plant willows and excavate the stone walls and the granite slabs, but it was still a gullion of sludge, just a cow-hole for Monsieur Aunay's beasts. The bank above was a snag of dead bramble, buckthorn and flailing whips of untrimmed ash, but I'd cleared halfway, tugging links of barbed wire fence from claws of grass where even the dirt was rusted. It was German Army wire, you could tell from the clips between barbs.

The helmet was under leaf-mould and lifted out

like a bowl, leaving a smooth hollow of dry, con-figured roots. The leather webbing was complete, snapping as it eased free. And there, like a coronet, still recognisable after fifty-two years, were woven sprigs of lavender.

For a second, this soldier was more real to me than Joy, sitting in the meadow with his helmet capped on the fence-post as he scratched his head and guzzled stolen cider, the farm behind him ransacked. He'd splashed himself in the *lavoir* and filled his can-teen from the trickling spring, ears drying in a stroke of summer. I held this rusty helmet with its Bosch-drop over the ear, picking out rust-wafers and sycamore leaves like fossils of extinct fish, running my finger round the bullet hole. He'd stood up, put the tin hat back on, the hole appearing as suddenly as the shot, straight through the daydream, killing him where the helmet fell.

I carried it back to the house at dusk, driven inside by the merciless cold. Because of the wind I was sleeping downstairs, rolled up in the duvet on the floor between the *armoire* and the woodstove, instead of adrift under the roof in our big empty bed. Up there the tiles slid away at night and splintered in the yard, like dreams of broken teeth. Even the glass out of the skylight took off and put a deep scratch down the side of the Land Rover.

The dark closed in and the moon shone hard as a mortuary light, flooding the room in formaldehyde sheen. I ate a bag of monkey nuts instead of cooking, and used the German helmet as a bowl for the empty shells. If I fell asleep before exhaustion the mice

21

would wake me, pulling at my hair, so I set this corral of wooden mouse traps called Lucifers round the floor and slept inside it, only they snapped all night. Or the geese at their watch would wake me, running round the yard like Nazis in a daze, confused by the moon or in a panic over the two-foot-long coypu who kept a den in one corner of the *mare* and emerged at night like a submarine.

For several nights a smell had curled up into the house from under the floorboards. But now it detonated just as I settled down, so I put my clothes back on over my pyjamas and thought okay, I'll rip the floorboards up.

I spent an hour smacking the torch in the barn as I looked for the jemmy, unable to strike matches in there because of all the US Army jerrycans leaking jeep fumes since 1944. Everything was black except this old goat skin nailed to the back of the barn door. The same door the Normans used to nail owls to in 1745.

I stepped on a rake and the six-foot handle smacked me under the left eye. I couldn't get the Land Rover started to use the headlights and even the split-charge terminal had rusted up in the damp so I couldn't run a spot off the lighter socket.

When I did get back to the house with the jemmy I couldn't smell the body at all. I hoped I'd dreamt it, only once the door was closed the stink unfolded twice the size. The problem was now obvious. To get the planks up I'd have to take the wood stove out and it was still alight. I opened the door and all four windows, kicked the smokepipe off and dragged and rocked the iron box across the clay tiles. It belched smoke and I had to wrap my left arm in a wet towel. When I reached the big granite fireplace the stove crashed on to its side. I'd forgotten to take the chimney panels out so the smoke spewed back into the room. I knocked the panels down and rushed outside half asphyxiated, waiting for the smoke to clear from the house.

Then I had to empty and dismantle the *armoire* because it was too big and heavy to move alone, which meant bagging Joy's clothes, something I'd been putting off. Once that was done I knocked the *armoire* pegs out and stacked the pieces neatly in the *grand séjour*. Next came the armchair, the table, the bookcases and some barrels we'd used as tables. The worst thing was this polystyrene sheeting we'd glued down to keep the damp and the cold out. On top of it was cheap blue carpeting tacked tight against the skirting. In spite of this the wind still got under there and the carpet billowed, in-out, in-out, like the floor was breathing.

It was 3.30 a.m. by the time I had the boards up and there were drifts of polystyrene swirling round the house, all charged with static and wind from the open door like a scene from one of those dozy plastic snowshakers I had in the sixties, a souvenir of Madame Tussaud's.

I stepped onto the bare clay three feet below the floorboards and found the body of our cat curled up in the corner. She must have crawled through the vent after a mouse or eaten a poisoned rat and crawled in there to die. It was me who'd put rat poison down. I hadn't minded too much when they'd gnawed holes in the night or even when I saw one run across the floor with an apple, only one night I woke to find a rat sitting on my stomach.

I put the cat in a bin bag and buried her in the wind and the dark as tears blew in my mouth and up my nose like flies. Then I sat at the table in three jumpers and two *joggings*, drinking coffee as the sun rose like a glint on the ice, the door still open, unable to see the point in putting anything back.

FOUR

Austen met me at the airport in his 1956 Land Rover
and we left Ray, Steve and Frogget arguing with
porters in the airport bar. Straight off Austen said:

— So you're Zan's boyfriend are you, bloke?
Well, she said I've got to keep you away from all
those Kuke dolly birds at the Starlight Club, ha!

A crate of Guinness rattled in the back along
with two sacks of maize, two hens tied by the legs
and *debes* of paraffin and water.

— They're for Wanja, he shouted over the
engine as we rattled across potholes towards the
Ngong Hills.

— Zan tell you about Wanja, bloke?

— What do you mean?

— I think she's gone mad. Bloody worrying,
bloke.

— Zanna?

— No, ha. Wanja. Round the bloody bend.
Those fucking Tanzanian witch doctors. She puts
bloody lipstick round her eyes and mutters to herself
all day. Found her walking round the *shamba* last
night, starkers. Says there's a devil in her stomach.
Wanjiku's running the place now. She's only twelve.
Can't go to school in case her mother burns the
place down.

It was probably the drought turned Wanja mad because a wind like a blowtorch scorched across the shadeless plain. The Ngong Hills looked desolate in the clear air.

— Lions still up there, bloke.

This was Masai country parcelled up and sold to Kikuyus who didn't already have an ancestral plot in the bush. Narrow strips of land still shadeless between rough homesteads. Umbrella thorn and clumps of candelabra where Masai cattle grazed on the unenclosed land. Grey-black cotton-soil sloped up to the hills patrolled by kites and eagles.

In Austen's compound the rainwater tanks were empty and the earth was cracked. Wanja was in the *shamba* tying strips of cloth and ribbon to withered stalks. She wore an anorak despite the heat, hair uncombed and dusty. An ex-prostitute Austen had 'rescued' from the tourist bars, now she was singing a Kikuyu hymn as a big old white drake with goiters and sores stumbled round her.

Austen told her he'd got the chickens but she just stared and shrugged. He untied them and they ran round the compound. Wanjiku looked like a mission-school house-girl with dusty knees, short white socks and grey cotton frock. No one knew the identity of her father, just that he was one of Wanja's Johns from the Starlite days. Wanjiku curtsied and helped us unload the truck. There was a gas fridge in the storeroom and I guzzled cold water from glass bottles.

— Don't forget to boil the water first, bloke. Comes from a standpipe in the village.

It tasted of flouride and Wanjiku's teeth were stained from it. Inside, the hut was baking because there was no ceiling under the pitched tin roof. Austen said there were love birds nesting up there once, but the chatter drove him nuts so he'd chased them away. Wanjiku started sweeping the bare concrete floor round the tatty sofa and dusted Austen's desk which rocked against the shiplap walls. There were stacks of blue flimsy foolscap, a huge grey typewriter, a paraffin lamp, some rare books on a single shelf reserved for Africana.

I dozed in a corner all afternoon while Austen was away. Wanjiku crept about, peeled potatoes, filled the paraffin lamps. The roof clanked and the smell of baked creosote fumes gave me a headache. The sunset didn't linger into evening and Wanjiku lit the oil lamps and put the potatoes on the bottled gas stove. Austen came back with two oil drums full of water and I helped him drain them into one of the rainwater tanks which were sunk underground. I said I needed a shave and a wash.

— Piss on the saplings, bloke, and waste-water on the paw-paw tree.

Wanja came in to eat the fluffy boiled potatoes and bean stew with fragments of goat's leg. She started singing Kikuyu hymns and Wanjiku joined in.

— The Spirit of Zion Church, Austen said. I could throttle the fucker who put that up. Just a tin *duka* with a cross on it by the water tap. I say we go out bloke. Bring a sweater, it gets chilly.

He really wanted to take me to the Starlite or

the Pub, but he was being protective because he said
Zanna wouldn't approve.

— First day, bloke. Take it easy, ha.

We headed out through Masai country and came to
the Craze which was supposed to be an out-of-town
nightspot and hotel. The bar was empty and there
was one white couple on the disco floor, dancing
like it was a game of blind man's buff. Me and Austen
sat on twirly iron chairs with red, heart-shaped,
leather upholstery. On the menu was chips, fried
eggs, fried bread and baked beans: sixteen bob. There
was tomato sauce on the table and waiters in red
jackets lined up to shake our hands. When the white
couple saw us they came straight over and the disco
was turned off. They were brother and sister, the
bloke a slightly younger version of Austen, tanned
and wiry with a clipped voice like he'd been shouting
at natives all his life. The moustache was 1901. He
was repatriating himself, that's what he said. Eleven
years in Zambia. He banged his fist on the table.

— Why should I bother with that man? Eh? Tell
me that.

— Who? Kaunda? Austen said.

— Of course. The man's a fool. KK's done nothing in eleven years. Just sacrificed his socialist ideals
for a kilo of fucking sugar.

He was just as bitter about the Craze too. He'd
wanted a last fling, a stop-over in whore country,
but these Indian bastards had conned him into staying
at the Craze. They'd offered transport and said these
out-of-town weekend nightspots were trendy with

28

the new middle-class African and enlightened Europeans. His sister had come out to meet him for the
week and they were flying back together. She wore
an orange kaftan and kept saying: it's alright Robert,
it's cool.

She got the disco turned back on. The light show
was a bloke shaking a coloured bulb in each hand
like maracas. The four of us danced till Austen said
it was fuckin ridiculous and we left.

Wanjiku came running out the shack when we
pulled up. As Austen switched the engine off we
could hear a commotion, a wailing and crying in the
distance. It was too dark to see my hands. I could
make out a dim glow here and there half a mile off.

— Where's Wanja? Austen said.

— Oh Austen, Wanjiku said and started crying.
She say to tell you she has gone to Tanzania.

— Shit and derision! What's going on up there?

— I do not know.

Austen locked me in the shack with Wanjiku
and gave me an airgun. He let the Ridgeback loose
and set off on foot with a *panga*. I blew the lamps
out but what with the fear, the jet lag, the heat and
the sudden change of diet, my guts gave out. I had
five seconds to get to the long drop only we were
locked in. I could've gone through the window but
the dog would've shredded me. Austen came back
and found me washing my trousers in a bucket and
needing somewhere to stash the soiled pages of
yesterday's *Daily Nation*.

— Bloody drunkard, *mshenzi*. Not you bloke.

29

Up there. Josphat bloody Githinji. *Chang'aa* gang war. Four women with kids after Githinji's son start stoning old Mama Githinji. Whole family's running all over the *shamba* yelling like dogs. God! The police car's outside the bar. Two police, dead drunk, say they're not assigned.

He wanted to sit and talk now, to map out my career, to get me stringing for the BBC Africa Service. Him and Zanna had all the contacts. I didn't booze back then, or talk much. I just listened and gulped down Austen's Roosters, short lethal fags made of uncured tobacco with no filters. Austen shuttled between the sofa and the crate of Export Guinness in the storeroom, small bottles brewed under licence in Kenya. One flick of his well-worn Swiss Army knife and the bottle tops rattled to the floor. One Rooster, one Guinness, six or seven swigs a bottle till he became louder and maudlin while Wanjiku slept soundly on a mat on the kitchen floor.

Everywhere I suggested going for a story he said was too dangerous.

— Stay out of Uganda for the moment bloke. The Ministry of Defence just announced it: guerillas gonna resume bombing campaign in Kampala.

So I flicked through the *Daily Nation*. Teenage girls at Lamu jailed for idleness.

— Trouble there too, bloke. Three hour shoot-out between bandits and police. Killed two of 'em and arrested the truck driver. Indian smugglers. Three hundred and forty elephant tusks. God! Right fucking shambles this Wildlife bloody Army.

Kenyatta's bloody wife still flies about in an army helicopter massacring zebra with a machine gun.

I said I'd just hitch out to Naivasha then. A dispute between neighbours had turned into the serial buggering of chickens by rival gangs in Kakamega. Austen said I couldn't sell a story like that so why didn't I go interview a dentist about flouride in the water. And if Wanja came back I could ask her about skin-lightening creams. He said all the prostitutes used them to make their skin go pale. He reckoned it was the mercury in the cream that had turned Wanja mad.

My idea was different. I wanted to visit Joy and do a story on gold panning and cattle rustling. But I wanted to *be* something first, get the red dirt on my boots and find some connection for myself. Maybe my character would form itself in parallel to the story I found. I didn't tell him those bits, and I didn't ask him about Joy either, but I didn't have to wait long before he mentioned her:

— Hey bloke, I've got it. You must go and see this woman Joy up in Amolem . . .

I could've asked him what she was like but he was ratted on Guinness now and I wanted to preserve her welcome like it was a real memory, not a guess or a hope.

The Rooster smoke was coming out his ears as he banged the chair and shouted:

— D'you know what that cunt Mengistu does to the Ethiopian people? Charges the fuckers he shoots for the bullets.

I wasn't interested enough to listen now. I was

31

picturing Joy in her long months between visitors, the airmail envelopes crisp and yellow and filling with insect pepper, her despair if a guitar string snapped, sewing up the holes in her mosquito net with raffia, listening in the night for cattle raids and aeroplanes, snakes and shooting stars . . . Listening out for me.

— Hey bloke, Austen said. Zanna give you that bloody jacket for Schick?

It was in the bottom of my pack, a heavyweight camouflaged Barbour which I'd agreed to deliver, new and oily.

— Christ almighty, Austen said when I gave it to him. Bloke's gonna wear that down the Starlite? Mad bastard.

— Who is this Schick? I said.

— You don't wanna know bloke. Man should wear a Keep Away sign round his neck.

It took seven bottles of Guinness before Austen was pissed enough to go to sleep.

Next day I set off for Naivasha, fifty miles north, reaching Dagoretti by clapped-out bus. For the settlers of Karen/Nairobi, Dagoretti was where Africa began, with the last white homestead in sight of the township.

The streets stank of raw sewage and barefoot women carried bundles of firewood. Kids queued for water with twenty-litre cooking-oil tins. There were mud houses in the lanes, roofs made of flattened tin cans, doors from packing cases. There were barber shops in the market square and radio repair shops, charcoal sellers, bars and cafes. Women in brilliant white dresses walked home from church.

A few kids followed me up the long hill towards Kikuyu.

— Hey you. *Mzungu*. Liverpool, Liverpool. Where are you going?

At the top there was open pasture rising to a coffee grove. A gutted white mansion behind the spiked *muigoya* hedge. A boy was collecting the leaves in a basket so his family could wipe their arses.

— Good morning sir, he said. Have you come to live?

— No, I said, and he was crestfallen.

There were buses and taxis in the shabby township. I asked the boy which bus for Naivasha.

— Hey you, he said. You stay here and eat paw-paw. You go that way and those thugs there are the bad men. They will steal your bag.

— I must go to Naivasha, I said.

It was the middle of the afternoon and the township men were already drunk. Over the road, two North Yemenites were getting into a Datsun Cherry. I guessed they didn't live out here so I waved and ran across.

— *Salaam*.

They greeted me back, we shook hands. They wore brown nylon and smelled of tea rose, their teeth were brown and one of them smoked an imported cigarette.

— Which road are you taking? I said.

— The road to there.

The driver pointed out of town.

— Away? I said.

— Yes, away from here.

— Will you take me?

— Welcome, they said.

They'd been chewing *mirrah* and were cake-eyed, judging by the pile of stalks on the floor in the back of the car. They asked the usual questions, like was I a tourist? A German? Why did I go to Kikuyu Junction? For the girls? The beer? Had I read the Koran?

In situations like those I usually kept it quiet, head down. I'd met too many travellers on the overland route who turned up the volume and tried to make the cross-over. They chewed the *mirrah*, grooved on the Koran, in for the ride like pocket Kerouacs, but it always turned bad.

If I was undecided about being in Africa anyway, it was best to keep to dignity, respect, and manners. That was my travelling creed. It avoided confrontation.

My gift, my real talent, was to go through life invisibly. I could be the only white man seen for twenty years but still dilute any interest in my existence. Other travellers were like the Pied Piper or the UN turning up with a lorry-load of aid. The whole district flocks out the bush to see and touch them.

It was my first real day back in Kenya. Since I'd last passed through a couple of years back, an attempted coup had sharpened security. Now I had a year's open ticket, eighty dollars cash, and a couple of hundred shillings bummed off Austen till the end of the week. Khalid was a careful driver; his friend translated the Day-Glo quotes from the Koran on the fringed pendants hanging round the inside of the car. But we were only three miles out of Kikuyu Junction when Khalid said:

— Police. *Alhamdulillahi.*

It was a roadblock five hundred yards ahead, a blue Land Rover with light flashing, spikes across the road, rifles in the air. Without a second's pause, Khalid opened the glovebox, took out two small packets and tossed them onto the back seat beside me.

— I give you one hundred United States dollars for putting these into your pocket and for the talking. In English. No Swahili. Is very important. English. The police are scared of good English. I know this for ten years I live in Kenya.

I put them in my pocket because Khalid's logic was impeccable. There was no risk to me, whatever happened. I wouldn't be beaten up, jailed or face extortion, but they would. If the police searched me I'd tell the truth and be believed. The point was, we all wanted to get to Naivasha and this was the best solution. I needed a hundred dollars and they knew it.

The police waved us down. I leaned out.

— *Jambo*, the policeman said.

— Good afternoon, I said. How are you?

I didn't give him a chance to answer. He tried to lean in and take a look. He stank of millet beer too.

— How are you? he said.

— Very well, thank you. What's the problem? I'm taking my two friends to Naivasha to have tea with my mother. We're already late.

— Okay, he said. Go to Naivasha.

— Thank you. Goodbye.

The Yemenites were deadpan for a mile then praised Allah the Merciful. I handed back the packets and didn't ask what they contained and they didn't tell me. I saw one contained foreign exchange because they paid me from it, one hundred and fifty dollars US, a bonus of fifty.

— You, lucky charm, Khalid said.

— You could be professional, Jamal said.

— Will you do it again, one day? For us?

I knew exaggerating my own immunity would be dangerous, only the money was a good reason to consider it and I'd be free of Austen's political hand-me-downs. I still needed a source of foreign exchange to act as a reserve against local shillings. And I'd been given a value by these two Yemenites, the threads of self-definition, the first contour in my personality. I felt anonymous, but anonymity didn't just mean blending in with the *wananchi*. And it wasn't only my skin colour which was opposite, it was my polarity. I always seemed to be travelling or just flowing in the opposite direction to everyone else. I emanated this lack of interest, this *laissez-faire*. It could've made me the perfect smuggler, if I wanted to be one. But my vocation was to drift. I could wait five days sitting on my rucksack at the bus station in Dar es Salaam for the bus to Zambia. Or five hours for my rice and beans in the New World Eating Bar in

Wethefuckarwe. I didn't need profit to eat *githeri*, just five bob here, five bob there.

So what else made me the perfect smuggler's lucky charm? I could fake a plummy accent which wouldn't fool anyone in London but could strike notes of authority in Africa. I failed to interest people, even prostitutes and beggar boys ignored me. And I knew every border, road, dive and dodge in East Africa, or would do soon enough. I could multiply the briefest details into facts, like my whole being was a vacuum that sucked in single experiences rapidly and completely, expanding them by intuition. In this way, places I'd never visited were familiar; places arrived at never confused or disoriented me. Yes, I was ready to accept I was the perfect smuggler's lucky charm.

I wrote my name on a piece of paper with Austen's PO box number. I said I'd do it again if they needed me, as lucky charm, that is. There'd be no compromise in that. Then Khalid said:

— You want to sell your passport? One hundred dollars?

— Yes, I said, why not.

— Hey man, Jamal said. You know Mr Schick? You do good business with Schick because he want lucky charm . . .

Three weeks and one expensive fever later I went to pick up some new passport photos in downtown Nairobi. Embassy Jagger, photographer. His studio was a tin hut behind the market place, beside a ten-foot pile of rotting fruit skins. His choice of backdrop was either a grey sheet or plastic shower curtain. It wasn't my face on the photos. It looked like a carrier bag drying on the line, or a police identikit. I stared at the likenesses again for some sign of recognition. It was like he'd lost the film, or the camera hadn't worked so he'd taken a negative of a long thin Luo's face from his drawer, over-exposed the print and tinted up the grey. My big lips and flat nose, fluked eyes, pocks and a scar. My first ever photograph, hence the fear, pride and perplexity.

I sat in the New Protein Best World Cafe and forged Austen's signature on the back of the photographs then rushed to the High Commission to report my passport stolen and apply for another.

— Must we always have to tell people we close at 11.30 when it says so on the door!

— I need a fuckin passport.

He wouldn't even let me leave the photographs.

I was meeting Schick for the first time at three, against all Austen's advice. Schick needed a 'passenger' for a run into Uganda and I'd had a good recommendation from the Yemenites.

I thought I could kill some time in the park so I ran across to the traffic island, sprinting with the crowd as the buses heaved down. A packet fell from someone's back pocket and bounced on the ground. A split second and the haze and clutter of legs left it behind. I was at the back. My instinct was to scoop, lift and keep going in one movement like nothing had happened and no one had noticed. But my balance was barged sideways by a man who fell on the packet, a fluke snatch which made us both lose momentum. By the time we'd saved our skins and backtracked out the road and onto the island, the crowd had left us and we were alone.

He was grubbier than me in his cockeyed cowboy boots and twenty-eight-inch flares with the linings dragging on the ground. His wide-lapelled pin-striped jacket was ripped to shreds and had red plastic pockets sewn on to the old ones. The stiffeners in the butterfly collars of his flower shirt were slipping out like false finger nails. His teeth were brown. His eyes bloody pink.

— Run after him, I said.

The crowd began to disperse on the other side. The man hesitated, holding the brick-shaped envelope. I could see a five bob note through its cellophane window, then slowly he began to slide the packet under his shirt. We were now alone on the traffic island in Kenyatta Avenue. Two hundred Kenyans were gathering each side for the next rush across. They must've all been watching us. People shouted at me from bus windows.

— Hey *mzungu*, hey you . . .

But I'd become detached by those photographs, or disfigured by malaria. I didn't feel *mzungu*. I was snide, doing business with my companion. There was no doubt we were trapped in some kind of companionship now, so much so that he sensed my greed. He noticed the tear in my trousers, the grey smelly jacket. I didn't have any socks on. A ponytail lanked out from under my crooked straw hat. I didn't even have a rucksack, just carried my passport photographs in my hand like any Kenyan.

— Run after him, I said, scanning the crowds. Not for the owner of the packet, but to see who was looking at us, and how soon we would be swallowed up in the next wave.

— Give it back . . .

I pointed to a man running against the lights, dodging his way across. I was covering myself, that's all. My companion didn't move. The packet was secure under his shirt and his hands were free. The lights changed. He was of course entitled to test me out. As the surge began, he simply stepped into the road without looking back. The crowd behind me caught up and I was swept towards him. At the kerb I made a lunge at his shirt. It ripped in my hand.

— Give that money back, I said.

But he knew what I meant and I was powerless to deny it. I was saying give it back to *me*.

— No, man, five-five. Look, there is ten thousand shillings in it.

The packet was exposed through his ripped shirt. It was written on. 10,000/-.

I was disappointed. It wasn't enough. It was only one month's rent on a Karen bungalow, or four more months bumming round Kenya. The price of a guard dog or twenty dinners at the International Casino. For my companion it meant capital, profit, or months of the good life down the Baboo Night Club in River Road. If he kept the whole ten thousand it was a year's salary.

The man I thought had dropped the money was

running back. Perhaps he remembered the feeling of it falling out. I knew it wasn't his money, that it was a payroll, that they'd call the police and he'd be beaten up. He ran past so I set off after him, shouting, ducking traffic as the lights changed. Across the Uhuru Road he went, until a council gardener shouted for him to stop. I grabbed his hand, started pulling him back to Kenyatta.

— You've had your money stolen. Back pocket . . .

He was wearing a bottle-green corduroy jacket. Round face, short, squat, out of breath. He slipped his hand into his jacket and showed me a green wage packet.

— Not me, he said. This is all I have.

I walked back to the traffic lights.

— Pssst. Pssst. The silly cunt thought I hadn't seen him standing there. Even the Nairobi City Council gardeners were leaning on their tools watching the two thieves meet up again.

— Psst. You ran after the wrong man, he said. You, a fool, shouting like that you get me killed. Now we go. Split five-five. Five thousand you, five thousand me. Aieee you fool. Say sorry.

— Sorry.

— That is okay. We are friends.

He clutched the money through his clothes. I suppose he'd earned custodial rights, but my self-evaluation was declining. I'd overacted the part. I'd take a thousand bob now just to get gone. But why should he have the nine thousand?

— Where you going? I asked.

41

— Walk, he say. Look for place.

He was fiddling with the packet now and pulled out the chit.

— Look. Ten thousand shillings.

It said *Kenya Transport Co. Mombasa 6,000/-. Nairobi 4,000/-.* I could take my half to the Transport office and get the loser off the hook but I wanted to go to Tanzania one day. I wanted to give Austen five hundred bob. I had to pay three hundred shillings for my new passport. I found myself telling all this to my new friend, so he didn't think I'd betray him. I showed him more holes in my clothes and said I couldn't pay the doctor for some medicine and didn't even have any underpants. He said soon I would have a lot of money.

We walked to Club 1900. He hesitated.

— No way, I said and walked on.

He caught me up and started to jibber.

— It is our lucky day. One time, before, I found nine thousand dollars in Mombasa and bought a Volvo. Five thousand shillings, it is nothing to me. This is true, I have eighty thousand shillings on me.

He started to look ridiculous, a parody of suspicion, tracing and retracing his steps, peering off the road at any path or hideout. We were down among the wholesale shops, the dry goods, the Asian importers and office suppliers. Old Nairobi, low colonial stores, shoe shops, seamstresses, the smell of cotton and leather and printers' ink. Cool, tidy, dusty shops with atriums and balconies where gentle but highly strung Patels sat at colossal rolltop desks looking down into the shop below. I'd begun to go there to change my currency, just paltry sums like a ten-dollar bill, but I was always invited to draw up a chair under the ceiling fan to drink a Pepsi and to listen to their gripes about police harassment, bent customs officers, greedy relatives in St Leonards.

— Give me twenty steps, he said. I am turning off this road on the corner.

He pointed to a rubbish patch, a wasteland with paths that crisscrossed between the ditches and the warehouses. It was lunchtime. Workers lounged in groups, Asian shopgirls smoking and drinking tea, messengers in flipflops chucking mango skins in the gutter. They all watched as I waited for my signal. It came from a ridge a hundred yards away. He beckoned, like he was digging a hole with one hand, before squatting under banana fronds. A hundred people saw me pick my way over to the sewage drain.

— Were you seen? he says.

I felt sick. I'd used up a whole day's energy and shouldn't have been slagging on an empty stomach after two weeks throwing up chloroquine. My legs were too weak to squat and I got the shakes. He was waving the packet in the air.

— Your lucky day. My lucky day. Which day you born?

He gave me the chit. I was born yesterday.

— You destroy it. Tear it up.

I struck a match but he blew it out.

— No, just tear.

I tore it up and wanted to ditch it where it would be carried away on the flowing scum.

— Now just put it down, he said.

As I sprinkled the fragments he wanted me to squat. The notes were half eased from the envelope when I saw a man come over the ridge.

— There are some people, I said.

Now the man in the green cord jacket smiled at me.

— They've followed us, I said.

— Ah, he said. They are the police. Just sit here.

The man in the cord jacket smiled at me again and came across to shake hands.

— How are you? he said. We go to the police now.

I got up and followed him across the ditch and got wet feet. I was ushered under another banana bush with more urgency now. This was it, a beating, and I'd nothing to bribe them with except perhaps my jacket. We all squatted. Were the police already under the banana bush? I couldn't see the shop-girls any more. My companion showed them the money.

— Here, all of it. We are not taking any of it. It is all here.

— The cheque, the man in the green cord jacket said. The chit. Where is this?

He turned to me:

— Did you have any outside money?

We were both searched. Why was I so silent? There was no chit. Only my photographs which they handed round, then gave back. In my half-delirium I thought: why couldn't they see they were of him? Why couldn't they see I'd stolen his face.

— This man, my companion was saying. He didn't know. He is nothing to do with it.

They looked at me.

— That's right, I said, pointing to the man in the green cord jacket. Ask this man.

He said: this is true.

A policeman took me aside.

— I'm sick, I said. It was all I could say but it worked.

— You go now. If you come to the police station this man will change his story and blame everything on you. That officer likes your pen.

I gave him my metal Parker ballpoint and wondered, what would Joy think of me now?

FIVE

Until we found Le Haut Bois, me and Joy were
living on the campsite at Putanges. It was the summer
of 1994 when Normandy was green with rain and
convoys of old British Army trucks and American
jeeps that had come over for the D–Day fiftieth anni-
versary. Solemn old men in berets, *anciens combattants*
spattered in medals, saluted at war memorials lined
with bombshells painted grey. Shy Welsh boys
dressed like soldiers in fatigues stood outside cafes in
La Ferté Macé plucking up the courage to go in and
order a beer. The occupied French waved as we
drove by, just coincidence that our old green hardtop
was army surplus. We soon demobbed, but something between the exaggerated welcome, the false
wartime solidarity and the distorted mission of our
lives kept us there and we outstayed our welcome.

The bocage was like a parody of its own past
because every *commune* was a lost world. We drove
in and out of eras which had vanished without trace
in Britain. The past sat there like undrained land.
We saw farmyards unchanged for four hundred years
slipping into ruin, the creepers taking over, the discarded implements and machinery left where the
horse dropped dead or the steam bailer clapped out.
In corners of these yards, opposite the old farm-

houses, were the new *pavillons*, those beige rendered, fixed-price bungalow kits the old couples had always dreamed of since the war. The farm sat like the rubbish now, strewn in the yard and on the land, waiting for ruination.

The campsite was a one star municipal but by July it was like an overspill from the ZUP and HLMs, the council flats of Falaise and Argentan. Family caravans linked with orange awnings, the TVs on all day, the men still going to work in the Moulinex factory. In the evening they'd be in their tattoos and yellow shorts, bonnets up on smoky Simcas, revving up while their fat wives tipped bags of crisps into bowls and fetched sticky bottles from striped orange kit-chenettes. Their dogs pissed up everyone's wheels and their cats were kept on bungee leads skewered to the ground.

We were pitched under an old beech tree twenty yards from the river Orne for seven francs a day. It seemed like the right place for Joy to forget Africa, at least till she decided where she wanted to go next. She'd sit outside under the beech tree reading while I went perch fishing in the gorge below the dam at Rabodanges. In the evenings we'd boil our tinned *ratatouille* on the petrol stove and eat goat's cheese with cider from the farmer's barrel. Then we'd stroll slowly round the village, almost door to door, like we were counting the stones on the walls, smelling the omelettes and the onion soup. We talked to cats and little girls and nodded to stubby farmers tumbling out the Bar des Sport. We lingered with our beer at the Pot d'Etain where the *patron* had a handlebar moustache as big as a ferret and all his cycling trophies were in a row behind the bar.

One evening we were in the Grande Rue, a narrow curving street with tiny stone houses built round boulders big as the rooms inside. The backs plunged two storeys down to gardens which ran alongside the river. We could see them from the campsite, like an escarpment, or cave dwelling. One of the houses was a small dark office with the round, gold sign of a notaire hanging like a monocle from the wall. In the window there were faded colour photocopies of old farmyards, *corps des fermes*, hovels and ruins, all from a time-warp. Nobody wanted them and the pictures had faded out until you could hardly see the prices. They read like old money, two, three, four thousand pounds. No toilet, no water, no telephone. No comfort, it said. But there were bread ovens, oak beams, cider presses, rabbit hutches and kitchen gardens, cellars, attics, wells, springs, cider-apple trees, pear orchards, bee hives, stables, pig-houses and smokeries.

We toured other villages looking for these part-time *notaires' études*, one dusty window, the gold paint peeling off the hanging sign. We found more faded ruins and half the houses in these villages had an *A Vendre* sign nailed on the front door like a wreath for the dead. We peered through crusted windows into kitchens with stone sinks, post office calendars for 1968, black and yellow linoleum, straw chairs with half the legs gnawed off by woodworm. There was always a neighbour fussing over potted fuchsias round the step, sweeping our footprints away behind us, hanging the wet floor-cloth from a nail.

Old women in housecoats and cardigans came out to tell us they didn't know the price, or if they did they said four million old francs.

We bought survey maps and drove all day after cheap houses. We found them along dusty brown lanes which crossed courtyards and wound between barns and cider orchards and pasture. Hamlets where every house was made of mud and lay empty, the grey net curtains like dead eyes, dried up flies caught along their edges.

At some point we should've asked ourselves what we were doing, who we were, what we expected to become by slipping into skin shed by dead peasants. Until, one evening we drove out to Le Haut Bois, looking for the *fermette à rénover* we'd seen advertised in a window, with outbuildings, 4,964 square metres of land, pasture with pear trees, 85,000 francs. We saw a bicycle leaning against a statue of Our Lady in the hedgerow, a little man in blue overalls slashing the grass along the verge, flattening the buttercups and cowslips. Joy said we were looking for the place that was for sale. He scratched his head and looked at the nearest hovel sticking from the brambles and vines. That's for sale, he said, and so is that, and that. Half of the *commune* was for sale. Everyone was dead.

— Do you want to buy a house?

— Yes, we said.

The first time we'd admitted it.

— You're going to live here? he said.

— We do live here, Joy said.

*　　*　　*

49

By August we were lodging in the Grande Rue with Widow Cardonel while hesitating over signing the promise to buy Le Haut Bois. Madame Cardonel was so old her skin hung like a curtain. She dressed in black and put all her remaining strength into polishing cold metal, ringing out dishclothes and pouncing on infractions of the rules.

Our room was upstairs and faced the river. We had the big brass Cardonel marriage bed but she'd locked every drawer and cupboard, taken the candles from the Virgin's votary and told us not to run any taps. She lived downstairs, sleeping in the front room. She rose at six, took a nap in the afternoon and went to bed at 9.30 like clockwork.

She called me *le monsieur*. My job from the outset was the fetching of water from the river in different coloured buckets. Blue for the washing-up, red for cooking, white for personal. Drinking water came from the supermarket. She allowed us one bath a week in the same water. One morning I eased the tap on in the upstairs bathroom to brush my teeth, but Madame Cardonel was banging on the ceiling with her cane before I'd even wet my toothbrush.

A nurse came once a week to give her a bath. I'd fetch one bucket and hoist it onto the bottled gas to warm, not boil. The nurse sponged her down in a galvanised trough in Madame's bedroom. Joy asked her why she didn't use *eau de ville*. The river *is* water, she said.

We cooked for ourselves, but Madame laid three places in the kitchen on the plastic tablecloth with its scenes of pots and pans. She'd use her hand like a snow plough on the table, chasing all the bread-crumbs into her palm when she'd finished her meal, licking up the crumbs till they were gone. And, when the milk was finished, she'd cut the box with scissors and scrape the milk dew off the insides into her cup. At night she never put the lights on, shuffling about with a little square bike torch she kept in a housecoat pocket.

Joy did the talking in French. I was still picking up words, like banknotes in the wind. I didn't know which to start on, chasing one too long and letting the whole sentence blow away. This meant that Madame Cardonel stopped looking at me when she spoke. She'd tell Joy that the monsieur hadn't fetched the water yet, or could the monsieur change the gas bottle. If she did address me she never waited till I processed what she'd said, she just snapped: *comprend pas, hein, comprend pas l'monsieur*. Every evening she nagged down a tumbler of *apéritif maison* and said: *that's another the Boche won't get.*

Sometimes the phone rang. It was rigged to the old bell from out the fire station so she could hear it. If we were in she'd say a man was coming at half-past five and we should wait in our room. It was business, she said. We'd listen to muffled voices coming up the stairwell through the closed kitchen door. Madame Cardonel chuffing down the steps out back with her keys, the unjailing of the *cave* door, locks, chain, padlocks. Five hundred bottles of Calvados the Germans didn't get. Some of it was seventy years old in the bottle. She put the 350 francs she got for each bottle in a biscuit tin under her marriage girdles in the *armoire*.

According to her, every farm we looked at as a potential home was never any good. Each time she'd say the man's mother was a *collabo*, she'd 'knitted with the Germans', and after Liberation the patriots went round the farms and shaved the hair off women like her. So when we told her we'd finally decided to buy Juliette Macé's old place at Le Haut Bois she shook her head and said: *huh, Aunay, he won't want you there.*

Monsieur Aunay came into the yard the day me and Joy moved into Le Haut Bois. It was September and the mud felt like putty and smelled like school clods off football boots. We arrived to find a pall of smoke in our neighbour Prodhomme's field and his 15-year-old boy backing a hay trailer up to our front door for a second load. Prodhomme just waded into the house and slumped anything he could carry for the fire, its black swirling smoke and orange flames, all Madame Macé's rag and bone sheething through the apple trees. We stopped them ransacking more, and Joy told them we'd bought the buildings *and* their contents. They were ashamed, that's all. Prodhomme had waited twenty years to get in there and clear up. Wiping out the traces of generations of Lecoeur, Legrange and Macé with a ketchup of diesel and a few broken matches.

We began to clear the rubbish from the house ourselves, wearing masks against the dust and smell, and new blue boiler suits we'd bought from Bricomarché. Suddenly Monsieur Aunay was standing there, red checked shirt, blue work trousers, the back of his hands raked with bramble scratches. We thought he'd come to welcome us. Joy said *bonjour monsieur* very properly, even rolling her r's and getting half the roll stuck in her throat. He ignored her and looked at me, said something I didn't understand, but mentioned Madame Macé. I smiled stupidly and tried mustering the vocabulary to offer him a drink of cider from the old crusty bottle cooling in the rain butt. Then Joy's grin changed shape and she rolled her eyes.

— What did 'e say? I said.

— It doesn't matter, she said.

He spoke to her now, asked if she spoke French.

— Yes, she said.

He repeated what he'd said and walked off, put his white crash helmet on and went up the lane on his old Solex.

— Well? I said.

— He said we weren't respecting the memory of Madame Macé.

SIX

Joy had been gone ten days when the police parked down on the lane below Le Haut Bois and walked up, tacking through the mud in shiny shoes. *Gendarmes, Brigade de Briouze*, it said on their van. It was 10 a.m. The taller one had tiny feet and carried the crime case. I made them coffee, just the warmed-up sips I'd poured back into the pot over the previous days. The room temperature was four degrees, the stove unlit. The case was opened and the *pandore* put on the latex gloves and powdered two glasses for fingerprints.

I'd fixed up the break-in myself, through Yannick Thiboult, a *brocanteur*, a junk wheeler who still owed us ten thousand francs. He'd turned up in his van one afternoon in our first winter at Le Haut Bois, one of those days when the landscape is like wet newspaper and the mud follows you indoors. Yannick was nosing, like anyone who came down our lane. Me and Joy were hacking plaster off the ceiling, gutting the *grand séjour* to expose the beams, when we heard the van. Days could pass and all we'd hear was a moped whingeing through the mist, the postman's yellow van at midday, a school bus, the toot of the bread van once a week. There were tractors, and the Paris–New York Concorde hitting the sound barrier at five minutes to five. So when we heard anything in the lane we'd stop, listen, and hold our breath like it would crash or it was an animal sniffing us out.

Yannick was standing in the yard hitching his trousers up. He looked like a kid pushed into something he didn't want to do. He saw the English number plate on our vehicle and started looking at the barn roofs and the treetops. He called behind him: *eh, Gilles* . . . Gilles came round the side, lighting a stub on his lip, flick-knife on the belt of his black leather trousers, matching black hair larded flat over a face like a grindstone.

Joy still did all the talking, but I was beginning to pick up a word here and there. They were looking for *les auges*, old granite troughs. Yannick must've noticed we had barns full of *camelote*. He was standing by one *auge* which had sunk to its rims on the edge of what might once have been a garden. Gilles was already trying to lever it out with his spinning-wheel fingers. Yannick offered us a hundred francs. Joy was a tough dealer. She'd stand her ground, pull her sleeves down, hook a thumb through the hole and talk with her hands like she was a French widow weighing melons. We had six *auges*, so Yannick knew we must have six of everything else. Le Haut Bois was like a museum.

He said his client was a Parisien, a *mine d'or* but an asshole. She would pay a thousand francs cash for the big *auges*, five hundred for the small ones, then stick them in her garden and set them up with supermarket geraniums. Joy said *moitié-moitié*, fifty-fifty.

All this time I was wondering what the pendant round Yannick's neck was, jigging on a chain. It looked like a big bearded face made of gold-painted tin, the top off a jelly mould. Gilles was brushing greenery off his trouser leg. He wasn't dressed for agricultural tackle collecting. He was a towner, probably from Flers, but Yannick was dressed from a bin bag left at the clothes recycling bin, grey *joggings* with knees like camel humps and a green acrylic jumper with pulled threads.

Five of the *auges* were too heavy to lift, even with four of us. So as Yannick backed his van round the yard and burnt his clutch, we levered each *auge* out with these eight-foot iron bars we'd found in the cider barn. Then with planks and rollers we'd heave and drag them into the van till it sagged in the mud. It was nearly dark when we finished. We sat at the table for a *coup*, a home-brew winter warmer. Everything Yannick saw, he asked how much, saying he'd just opened a *brocante* in the old primary school at Ste-Honorine. Ste-Honorine was a one-horse-trough village seven kilometres east with a tractor mechanic, a church and a *boulangerie*. There were mud houses where old women still slopped out, and a stray dog running across the road with a chicken in its mouth.

We'd seen his *brocante*, L'Atelier de Merlin. He'd hung two old chairs from the brackets of his upstairs windowbox and draped a hand-painted banner across the road. It looked like the place had shut down years back, but he was just waiting for his enterprise loan to come through. Even his van was rented. I wanted to let him in the barns but Joy didn't. Gilles kept asking Joy where she was from, why didn't she smoke, when was she going to have children. Yannick wanted to know if Scotland was a good place to find *camelote*. Him and Gilles were going there next month. I didn't believe a word of it. We got two hundred quid for the *auges* though.

On the day of the break-in I was supposed to stay out from midday till bedtime. I did a sausage and chips at Leclerc in Argentan followed by a weekly shop which I managed to spin out till 4 p.m. The shopping was an emotional gamble. Just three weeks before, me and Joy had gone Christmas shopping there. It had been so cold that day the condensation drips inside the Land Rover froze into rivets of ice. Joy's hands were blue inside her mittens and I felt sick. When we'd got home Joy said: *what are we going to do? We can't go on like this.*

I'd begun to frame everything she said in my own scheme of things, like those template marker systems for multiple choice. For my own peace of mind 'what are we going to do?' meant: how are we going to get warm? 'We can't go on like this' meant: we must get proper firewood. I still thought we were brave and authentic in letting ourselves slip down the evolutionary scale. From benefits to hunter-gatherers and, by that winter, scavengers. By nightfall on our last few days together, the cold was dangerous, minus sixteen. Our firewood pile was scrap from dumps, hedgerows and collapsed buildings. It had nails, rusty iron hinges, staples and barbed wire in it. It was frozen now and weighed twice what it should. It snapped the teeth off our chainsaw so we couldn't cut it to size for the stove. Instead, we made an inferno in the open fireplace, pulled up our stolen armchairs and cooked on trivets and cauldrons.

So I had no appetite for buying food at Leclerc that day. My trolley looked like the one parked near the exits, the one with the cardboard sign tied on with string: Red Cross, give a tin to the poor. Gone were the falafals and yoghurt, the corn pone bread and salads of marriage. In came the tins of sauerkraut, cheap blended wine in consigned litre bottles, tinned fish and tinned peas. I scooped up two bags of potato chips big as coal sacks.

I turned into the yard at midnight, expecting just a smashed window and some paltry disarray, but Le Haut Bois had been ransacked. It was like the house had regurgitated the previous hundred and fifty years, turned all the treasure it once contained back into rubbish. It looked just like it had the day we'd moved in, Juliette Macé's sick-house, the windowsill rotting beside her bed, rats gnawing on the floorboards, mouldy black slug trails across the plaster and that sweet, deathly cloying dry decomposure.

I just sat there listening to the slush drip through broken slates into tin bowls on the floor above. The cobwebs were black, the plaster walls pale mint green, that same cold luminous camouflage paint left behind by the German tank divisions. All over the bocage you could see chicken-shed doors and front gates and plaster walls all painted like tanks. And that's what it felt like then, Le Haut Bois smashed up by Panzers again. The wind shunted wet through the smashed window. Our books were tumbling down the steps outside getting soaked, glass in fragments under the window, the fridge on its side in the mud, our tools packed hurriedly into it and spilling out. The door was open, all the pictures were on the floor and the fucking table was gone. Woven into all of this were the archives, papers, documents and belongings of six generations.

I picked up this photo of Juliette Macé. She'd meant nothing to me before then. A widow picture this one, 1977, face like a mashed potato, black-ringed eyes, hair falling out. She disgusted me, I could smell the piss in her bed. I'll never forget going into her bedroom that day we moved in, the black smoke still belching across the orchard like they were burning her body. Her bedroom had been a dead end in anyone's life, sick-bed on castors, ten-ton walnut with an iron frame bolted in. There was a chrome, folding dressing screen toppled on the floor, lino glued to the oak boards, bottles of water from Lourdes dumped like a drunk, the mother of God's plastic face, solemn even in fluro-glitter, face down in the corner. Juliette's bamboo walking stick had split at the round handle like an alligator head and a boxed electric iron from the late fifties held the door open. A yellow plastic string mat on the bed, a cardboard box of milk analysis slips with dozens of unused ampules of beasts' antibiotics on top of them.

She'd had the water connected so she didn't have to use the well pump which was bolted to the wall, but here was no sink, just a granite slab with a lip, a hole in the wall and a stone shaped like a spout so the water ran down the outside then back in under the foundations. There'd been no phone, no toilet, no fridge, just an old Boreal gas cooker and a wood stove. We found her kitchen exactly as she'd left it in 1989. The clay tiled floor, the brass standpipe tap, the pine table knocked up out of military trailer boards, limping on worm-punched legs, her pile of invalid's rot stacked to the ceiling. Unwashed plates gravied together, mildy handbags, weekly copies of *L'Orne Combattante*, plastic baskets of fake wicker, a nylon headscarf, shoes with square heels which cracked like biscuits. Formica panels hung off the wall on one screw above the granite slab. Under the tap was a bowl and salad shaker, and a biscuit tin full of land-tax receipts dating back to 1946. Behind the door to the loft was the rope she'd tied round the veal calf's neck. Dangling on nails banged wherever she'd found a space were rusted paraffin lamps, buckled cycle wheels, bell-shaped beehives of woven rushes, cheese moulds, clogs, animal traps. Under the almost vertical loft stairs, the floor was wet sandy mud and the hexagonal tiles had been lifted. Beneath all this rubbish, the boots and shoes and walking sticks, the empty sardine tins, bottles, scraps of wood and cardboard, we'd found the Calvados, twenty pre-war bottles with black string tied round the necks, the corks eaten away by woodworm, the bottles splayed and rolling like nine pins. Me and Joy had guarded them like Madame Cardonel had guarded hers, but now they were gone. The burglars were supposed to have left them alone.

★   ★   ★

The plan had been to call the gendarmes in Briouze immediately, but the phone had been nicked too. I felt like driving there, giving myself up, confessing to a war crime, a string of violations against six generations. Le Haut Bois had been passed on to me with its past intact and now I'd let history down. This was more than domestic violence, worse than anything the Germans did in 1944. Worse than anything Aunay could accuse me of in respect of Madame Macé.

I went to the phone box at St-André and had to strike matches to dial the number. The mayor wanted streetlamps for nine inhabited houses; five of them voted National Front. The coin dropping in the box probably woke the whole village. The woman with the moustache put her light on and tried to see who I was. She spent her days leaning on a broom looking at the cemetery across the road.

The police said they couldn't come out till the morning. In the meantime I was to touch nothing, like I should rope off the scene of crime and sit in despair with the doors and windows open and the sleet howling through. Okay, so I sat there and thought of it as Juliette Macé's house because it didn't feel like mine any more. I mean what kind of farm was it where no one had thrown anything away since 1817? Where this bedridden Juliette had let the roofs collapse around her, refusing help, cleaning nothing. She'd let Prodhomme in to switch a heater on in the mornings and turn it off again at night, but she'd let the yard flood, the barrels floating up the walls, telling him to clear off if he came to drain it.

I picked out another photo and lit a candle to study it by. This time it was a 1930s oval sepia portrait of Juliette and her husband Marcel. Juliette wears her wedding ring, her Sunday coat with fur collar and cuffs, dark hair flat and held to one side in a long barrette. Her jowls and chin are round as a dinner plate and curve from ear to ear. Her expression's an anxious one and she looks no farm girl, too many dreams and headaches. You can see the nail on her left thumb's bitten short. You can see the buttons on Marcel's flies. He wore the same Hitler moustache his whole life. His short leather jacket is tight just below his waist with a big diagonal zip like someone tried to cross him out.

There was something missing from all the photographs of Marcel and Juliette. No children. They died childless. I'd never wanted children, but Joy had said that children were the only thing likely to bring Le Haut Bois back to life. So, like Juliette, I was the end of the line, denying the place a second chance, then trashing it. Maybe I should've just burned it down that night and accepted how deeply into their distorted lives I'd fallen. But this is hindsight. If there was one thing I'd learned in Africa, it was my blind tendency to live close to lives dedicated to self-destruction.

PART 2

SEVEN

Schick didn't need that Keep Away sign. In his disguise he stuck out in the crowd of tourists packed round tables outside the Thorn Tree. I went straight up to him, sat down and said: Schick.

A few miles south of the equator, eighty degrees in the shade, and there he was wearing the camouflaged XXXL Barbour Northumbrian, stetson, combat trousers, cowboy boots and *Easy Rider* shades. Only when he stood he measured about 5'4" on the flats of his feet, a bit taller in the chunky heel. His beard and shoulder-length hair made his disguise more impenetrable. Jemmy the stetson off and he was bald as a turkey buzzard. His face was pocked from bad food or disease and he thought he was a confederate general .or in *Apocalypse Now*.

— The jeep's over there, man, he said.

He drove us out on the Kiambu road where he lived in a tea planter's bungalow with six-inch 'toothpicks', knives, drawn in every window, on account of the 'cargo'. He wouldn't say just who was after him but he kept his *panga* blades smeared in solutions of iodine, vinegar and DDT. Treble whammies, he called them. Schick himself was such a triple-extra-large hoker that every talk with him was a sleigh ride.

— Makes the cut fuckin sting, he said. I'm tellin

ya, ya can chiv a *kaffir* to the bone and he keeps comin. But sting him and he cries like a baby.

The wind blew over the tea nurseries for miles and the only sign of life was a plume of smoke below the Mololo Hills. If the usual gang of thieves came for him he wouldn't stand a chance. He must've haunted himself day and night, trusting no one:

— *Mzungus*'re all up to their goddam eyes in *kaffir*-cunt. The *kaffirs* steal your piss to put on their *shambas*. They know I'm doing good runs. Listen, ninety thousand shillings in Uganda now, a Land Rover wheel. In six months a bottle of cognac's gone up from six to twenty thousand shillings. A kilo of weed's still only two hundred shillings. Running dope's a dream, man, but you need some brass knuckle-brain, someone to sleep chained to your jerry cans . . .

He didn't really have to go into Uganda to buy his *bhang*. He just fancied some civil war and was too scared to go alone. So what did he want me to do, dig the sap?

Schick was living in a hall of mirrors where everything was a box of tricks. His Kuke squaw was a pal of Wanja's who went on the game when he was away, leopard skin, red spikes, plastic hair. When I went up there Schick and Zipporah had put their guns on the table and Schick was complaining that Zipporah wouldn't make her Johns put a sock on it. AIDS had arrived and it was a load of *jok*. She liked it 'live', BBC – body to body contact. She said you don't suck a sweet with the wrapper still on.

— She does it for birdseed, man. One sample a night, just for good times and a Johnnie Walker.

Zipporah without beads and dreadlocks looked like the *shamba* lady she really was, growing maize and sweet potatoes, keeping chickens. She cooked the rice and beans on charcoal on the kitchen floor while Schick sat at his saloon table surrounded by pots of lacquer, glue, coils of rope and cheap plastic objects from Khalid's Seven-Up Import Stores. Ashtrays, mugs, vegetable peelers, lamps, vases, bottles. He sloshed on glue and wrapped them in rope, soaked them in dope then lacquered them. They dried in the sun and he tied luggage labels on them. *Hand-made for the orphans of Uganda by the Sisters of the Holy Cowpoke Mission for Uganda, in Kansas, Illinois.* He always took a joke too far. They were wrapped in paper and stowed in grocery cartons. At road blocks he'd just open one of the boxes and they'd believe he was a missionary. He must've practised on the furniture when he'd first dreamt up the scheme because all his lamps, chairs, tables, knife-handles, galvanised buckets, toilet and empty bottles were all roped and lacquered.

— Well, he said, what do you think?

I was thinking Schick was a nut and his scheme was a death-trap. I was thinking that Schick and Austen belonged in a museum or some Bush Stiffs Hall of Fame.

— Yeah, I said. It looks good. I'll do it.

Zipporah slipped a bowl of *githeri* in front of him like she'd boiled the beans in strychnine. Her face was purple from the mercury poisoning. Schick kicked a chair out from under his table.

— Sit. Eat. Zipporah, beer!

★ ★ ★

The border at Malaba was like a scrapyard. The drivers lounged on prayer mats, drinking tea under the shade of their trucks. Transit Goods from Mombasa, East African Roadways Nairobi, TMK Zaire, Dar, Burundi, Transocean Sudan, Kampala, Inter Freight Juba. Schick stayed in the pick-up, boots on the dash, Steely Dan tape raking through the cab. I changed the money round the back of the Safari Lodge, like turning a pound of butter into a pallet of bricks or armfuls of bogrolls. My handy-pack of Kenya shillings became four carrier bags full of filthy low-denomination Ugandan rags all dunked in the same oil, grease and dust which lay under the mile-long jam of baking Toyotas and a hundred glistening trucks. Schick locked the cash in the cubby under the passenger seat.

— I'll get you a Sprite, I said.

— Get me an egg and French fries.

Schick had a cigarillo going with his hat low over the eyes. His idea was to actually fill the back of the pick-up with grass, *bhang*, about six inches thick, then throw a few old banana leaves and bunches of *matoke* on top. We'd drive into Uganda as missionaries with lacquered goods, and drive out as fuckin gardening contractors. Seeing as he could load the pick-up full with *bhang* for about thirty quid it was worth the risk. It's just that he didn't need to go into Uganda to either find it or buy it cheap. Me, I needed the five-hundred-dollar pay Schick promised and besides, Austen had said that all foreign journalists had been booted out of Uganda and the World Service wanted anything I could get. They were even beginning to think I was a bit of an authority on it.

— We don't wanna look like Cuban mercenaries in a stolen pick-up, I'd said.

— Hey fuck, Schick said. Scare the ass off 'em.

— You wanna scare the ass off 'em Schick, the way to do it is in a clean white shirt with me in the cab talking BBC English. After the *jambo* shut yer trap, you know? No Swahili, let me talk. Just offer the cigarillos with a smile.

I'd discovered Schick was a reluctant loner, so bragging to himself was too much like speech therapy. He used to run his *bhang* into Sudan through Lodwar with his white girlfriend and a rifle he never used. She'd done *mirrah* to Somalia with him too and they got their dope out to Italy through Mogadishu. He had links with all the aid agencies specifically for this. Anyway, it was since his white girlfriend had dumped him he'd really gone all Serpico and quasi-militia. Blew his confidence I suppose.

I'd said no guns, no intoxicants, no prostitutes, no heroic driving.

— What fuckin else, man?

— No farting, I said.

The fact was I didn't believe in him. I didn't believe that any of his multiple disguises concealed more than a dwarf with a squeaky voice. The scruff hid a weak chin, the baggy fatigues a pigeon chest and chicken legs. The Fistful-of-Dollars voice was just a handful of change. He stank, he was ugly, he was all self-parody. If he'd just once put his boots

69

on the table and said shit, I'm a loser but what the fuck, we'd've all loved him and he could've chucked the NATO greasepaint in the trash. But he didn't, so you had to assume he was on a suicide mission.

Austen called him a freelancer, a bounty hunter. No fixed occupation, a roper as opposed to me who he called a stringer. But people baffled Austen unless he had a hand in their make-up. He could simplify me for his own peace of mind. I was his wife's bloke, someone to pass experience down to. His generosity was as reckless as his character assessment, but I didn't piss his shillings in the dust or steal behind his back so he was naturally worried when I told him I was going into Uganda with Schick.

— Christ bloke, he'd said. Schick's a nutter, bloody *shenzi*, bloke. He'll end up in Luzira prison. He's already told someone at the consulate he's going to Kampala to kill Obote.

The Nairobi train was in. Passengers walked the last mile to Ugandan immigration. Money touts stood in the open, Ugandan bankrolls big as logs stuffed down their expanding nylon socks. The old East African Railways line still crossed into Uganda behind the police posts. Foot *magendo* passed back and forth unchecked. Kenyan cyclists with stacks of white loaves balanced on the mudguards. Women staggered over with bundles of *kangas*, sacks of sugar and drums of cooking oil. Boys with cartons of 200 cigarettes.

The New Safari Lodge was cooking chips and eggs. The walls were pink with blue zebras and banana trees, a cassette player big as a suitcase belched hi-life, its bandoleer of Chinese batteries hanging out like pig entrails. I took a plastic plate of breakfast out to Schick. It had bloody splats of Peptang Barbeque Sauce the way he liked it. The traffic wasn't moving so I ate mine inside with the flies. In a moment I'd walk down to the police post with some Rothman's. I'd show some papers if they wanted. There'd be no trouble this side. They'd suggest we should stay in Kenya. Uganda was full of bad men. Then I'd stroll over to the Uganda immigration post, just to see who was in the hut. Hand the fags round. Make sure they knew I was a teacher in Uganda at the famous Mbugazali School. Look, here's my letter from Father Grimble on headed paper. Ah, they'd say, yes, Father Grimble. Very famous man in Uganda. And when we came to drive through he'd just wave to me like an old friend . . .

My dummy run was cut short. The well-worn phrase goes like this: *I thought it was a car backfiring.* So did everyone else. There was so much racket, I didn't even think it was a backfire, really. In fact I heard nothing, and I'm merely piecing it together. The drama had all been in Schick's mind, even if the shot was real. When I stepped outside, Schick wasn't there. I thought he might've just moved up and parked in some shade but the driver behind said Schick had suddenly turned round and driven back to Kenya in a hurry. He'd taken the plate and his knife and fork, and my pack.

I waited an hour and had to pay ten shillings for the plate and cutlery. I had to break into the emergency dollars in my money belt, do a hasty deal with a money tout and scuff up the railway line for the train with the last few stragglers and their sacks of Uganda coffee.

Next morning Austen drove me out to the tea plantation. Zipporah said that Schick had shot himself in the foot and was in Kenyatta Hospital. We found Schick's truck parked in the surgeon's slot, my pack still in the back under the tarp with the mission boxes. There was blood all over the driver's footwell and a bullet hole.

We found him sitting in the corridor on a nomad's neck stool, whittling some ebony with a bowie knife. Sitting like it was a hospital tent in Heroesville, his foot in twenty yards of field bandage.

— Smashed toes, he said. Bullet went clean through, man. Quinine Jimmie said I'm gonna limp for life. Hey, have to be a pirate now.

He was coming adrift on the morphine so there wasn't much believable or concrete in his rambling. I asked him why he dumped me and why the fuck he had the gun anyway and how he'd managed to shoot himself in the foot at all.

— That Zippy's got rubber lips. I told her to button it.

Schick said he'd dumped me at Malaba because he saw a mental picture of the two of us at a roadblock outside Jinja. We were being led away and shot by UPC Youthwingers behind a tree. He said this revelation was a gift of combat knowledge, years of scraping through. He said for a moment there I'd

72

fooled him, till this bolt of wisdom told him I was bad luck.

I'd completely lost sight of Joy because of Schick, so my next trip was out to Amolem, only to find Joy's house empty, the parched windows crusted blue with cobwebs on the inside. I'd imagined her sitting on an old sofa when I arrived, the goat hair stuffing hanging out, playing her guitar with the door open, teaching two Pokot girls a song, skirt rolled up above her knees, a skinny kitten hiding under a broken chair.

It was hot, early afternoon in Amolem, strips and stumps of shade in a vertical sun. I had an escort the mile from the road, six barefoot kids ran ahead through the dust and thorn bushes shouting as I trailed behind. They thought I'd come to Kenya to live in the *mzungu* house.

I thought it wouldn't have mattered if I didn't know what I wanted, who I thought I was, what I'd say. Joy would've done all that for me.

— Hey, welcome, hi, who are you? she'd have said.

So before I'd even met her she'd become imaginary and I spent the night in an empty house she'd just left. I knew the stale smell of her abandonment, the size of the emptiness she left behind, the shape of her dust, a pick of blood on a sticking plaster she'd changed before getting on her motorbike and riding away to Uganda. Next day as I walked out of Amolem the kids ran after me:

— *Mzungu, mzungu*, where are you going?

— To see Miss Joy, I said. In Uganda.

EIGHT

On our second try at the Uganda run we made
Kampala on a breeze. In six months security had
whittled down to thin air, so Schick insisted we play
safe and stay at the Kampala Speke with its UN
traffic and CD plates in the carpark, flower tubs, the
cool foyer, the supper table laid with silver. Schick
might've been a weirdo but he looked more the part
than me. He was used to pulling up in a truck and
swaggering over to a hotel desk with his car keys
and overnight bag and the money well stuffed in the
lining.

I waited outside. Schick didn't come back out
so after half an hour I went in looking like the
backpacker I was. Schick had already teamed up with
two Americans in the bar, cold beer froth on his
beard, tongue slapping round a crock of bullshit.
There was a colour telly on a plank in the corner
and I stood hypnotised. I'd never seen one in Africa.
A dim unfocused test card was held up by two hands
doing their best to stay concealed. UTV Channel 5.
The card was whipped away and the presenter stared
at us, trying not to blink, move, breathe. The pair
of hands shoved another placard in front of him and
the camera tried focusing. The music came on, a
gospel chorus singing: *Swing Low Sweet Chariot,*

coming for to carry me home. The placard said: *Help return stability in our country. Are you in the bush within or outside our border? Come out or come back home and join our happy brethren in the task of rehabilitation.*

That was a joke. Only 4 in every 1000 Ugandans owned a television. President Obote had lost control. His ministers were looting the treasury. The army was pillaging the country. The armed opposition, the rebels, weren't sitting in the bush watching this rubbish on TV. This was for the affluent elite, Obote's insiders, reminding them which side the bread was buttered. It meant: denounce your neighbour.

No one else was watching. Schick was breaking jaw with the Christian Aid roadies in their Grateful Dead T-shirts. They had a project of their own on the side. They'd bought these old gunboats which Amin had bummed off Israel to invade Tanzania from Lake Victoria. They were moored at Port Bell in Kampala, still had their engines but only cost five hundred dollars the lot. Castro the mechanic had two of the engines running already. I saw what Schick was thinking, that he could land his dope on the Kenya side at any little creek between Homa Bay and Kisumu. The roadies were planning fishing trips for rich American tourists and one of them had been a guide in Montana.

— I got a grand in tips a week, man. These assholes, they're all from New York. They just want you to tie their flies on, tell 'em where to throw it while you stand there and suck dick while they fuckin hook their fancy fuckin Orvis fishing breeches.

I went up to the desk, assuming Schick had

booked me in too. The receptionist was a president lookalike with his safari suit and two-faced welcome. I asked which room I was in and he said there were no rooms, that it wasn't a travellers' hotel. I pointed to Schick. The American gentleman, I was informed, had a room by prior arrangement, booked through his company.

I told Schick I was staying elsewhere, but he could book me breakfast. He barely paused to lick the beer off his lip.

— Good, *mzuri*, he said.

M-fuckin-*zuri*. When palookas like Schick started cutting their tongue with Swahili it was time to quit Africa. Once outside, among the limos and Suzuki jeeps and UN minibuses, I decided it really was.

There was an hour's daylight to come, the sun was still hot and sour. I walked past boarded-up shops, derelict offices, potholes and sewage in the road. I felt like an alien crash-landed on Planet of the Apes, finding a modern city sticking out the rubble. I longed for the smell of cut grass in the park, tame ducks, a bacon sandwich in sliced white medium with Branston Pickle. My search for Joy seemed ridiculous now.

Both Sikh temples said they weren't taking travellers any more. The immigration authorities had changed the rules. I suspected they'd got fed up with travellers kipping on the temple roof, smoking dope, shagging in their sleeping bags and pigging out on the free food. I tried the Habari Lodge but they said:

— Go and clear yourself at the police station.

You must go early, before the police are drunk and make trouble.

Kampala hadn't been that tense in months. Obote was on the radio announcing a curfew and appealing to the people: *what have I done wrong for you?* Outside, right on cue, a drunk policeman with his 'record book' said I should give him fifty shillings – protection money so he could buy *wargi*, moonshine gin. He wore a sick-stained white service raincoat. I walked away and he shouted after me:

— You are free by two.

At the next hotel the boy said:

— Tek me to England I am beggin you.

In Old Kampala people started rushing home to beat the curfew. Shopkeepers were loading their paltry stock into boxes to carry home, banging six-inch nails into planks over their doorways. People were running or driving crazy, up pavements and steps to cut two foot off the journey. In a square off Kampala Road an Asian storekeeper was shouting at two men with bows and arrows. One of them wore trousers with big yellow and black checks, the other a battered straw hat and a white rollneck fisherman's arran. They were the shop watchmen. The sign said: NEW DUAL SANITARY SUPERMARKET. The last time I'd been here this shop was a gutted ruin with sheets of scorched corrugated tin hanging over the concrete pillars from twisted fixings. Now it was a pink and yellow import store.

There were other Asians nearby, the ones Amin had expelled in 1972. The NEW DUAL had steel rolldown shutters and iron bars over the steel doors.

I ducked in to have a look while the Asian shouted at the watchman. English pre-packed food and dry goods. The bank rate was 360 shillings to the pound. The *kibanda* rate was 460 to 600. I wasn't buying a small packet of Golden Wonder Crisps for 620 bob or a Mars Bar for 300 bob. Four Bic chuck-away razors were 1,200. The Uganda minimum wage was 950 shillings a month.

The watchmen wanted to be inside the shop but the Asian wanted them locked between the steel shutters and the shop door.

— What am I doing for myself if I must pass water or soil? the watchman said.

— You think I'm stupid? I'm not locking you in my shop for eating and thieving . . .

The Minji Trading Store next door sold shirts for 8,000, Italian shoes for 50,000 and videos for one million shillings. This shopkeeper was loading all his stock into his car. He hadn't bothered renovating, he'd just swept the rubble out. The windows behind his iron bars were jagged glass.

The gunfire sounded in the suburbs a mile away. A beggar laughed at my turnups and I told him to fuck off. I started running, stumbling into craters and slipping on things I just did not want to think about. It was getting dark. There were no drain covers on the sewage channels and there were piles of rubbish waiting to be burned once they'd rotted. A boy ran past me saying:

— Sir you have just run near a *mshenzi* with a gun waiting to rob the by-passing citizen . . .

When I entered the ring of light thrown out by

the Speke I laughed out loud from fear and nerves. This time the night manager wore the safari suit. I explained the predicament and the man tutted.

— I can give you Baker's room for today.

— Baker's room?

— Yes sir. Baker is the general factotum for this hotel. He is departed to a funeral and is coming tomorrow.

I heard Schick's beery voice coming from the lounge.

— Ah, suck dick. How can Africans pronounce that!

Baker's room was in the service corridor. There was no lock and the door was just three planks of rough unpainted wood.

— Don't worry, the manager said. There are no thieves.

When he shut the door I felt like that man in my passport photograph, subverted and defaced. The room was twelve foot square with dirty pink washed walls, the old plaster staining through. The skirting line was painted dark green with Land Rover paint. The Uganda Coffee Board calendar nailed to the wall was seven years old and curled like fly paper. There was a portrait of Chairman Mao torn from a book printed in China. There were shovels and wood propped along one wall, and scuffed cardboard boxes stacked in the corner. This was all Baker had, I supposed.

I lay on his bed and looked at his clothes hanging from a nail. I'd never felt like a cockroach before when prying at other ex-pats' inner sanctums, but this time, staring at two torn shirts, a pair of ragged trousers and a floppy rinse-red hat, I knew I was insulting an African in my effort to deny my own racial advantage.

I put my radio on and listened to the World Service, an old recording from the archives about Virginia Woolf. Duncan Grant was recalling Virginia's glee from 1901, his white flannel voice already pee-stained: . . . *one day I mentioned the fact that I had a first cousin who'd been eaten by a bear, ha ha ha ha, and this caused unbridled mirth, and orrfen I was to hear, on Thursday evenings: do you know that Duncan has a cousin who was eaten by a bear?*

Perhaps it was those cardboard voices speaking in colonial copperplate which made me so hypercritical. I was unable to imagine what it was like to be Baker. At the same time I found it easy to be Duncan Grant.

I turned the radio off, grabbed my soap and walked into reception to ask where the bathroom was. There wasn't one. I'd have to use the facilities in one of my colleagues' rooms.

— Where does Baker wash?

— It is not necessary. I will get here one of your colleagues.

— No, I insisted, they're not my colleagues. Where do *you* wash?

— What is it you want?

— A bucket of water.

Maybe I thought I could wash the whiteness out of my skin, or that this African receptionist would be grateful for my solidarity. And five minutes later, washing myself in Baker's bowl, even in fresh dirty water, I still felt queasy and made sure I didn't have any black curly hairs on my soap after I'd put it down. And like he was testing me out, when I took the water back, the receptionist said something in Swahili I didn't understand, but the manner in which he said it was unmistakable.

In my pack I kept a Swahili grammar and excercise book. *Up-Country Swahili* it was called. *For the soldier, settler, miner, merchant, and their wives. For all those who deal with up-country natives without interpreters.* It was by F. H. Le Breton, first published in 1936. The long translation exercises consisted of authentic daily exchanges between natives and colonials. *Boy, my razor is spoilt, it will not cut even a little, I know you have used it to shave your head, and my scissors likewise, they are still dirty with your black hairs . . .*

Next morning the World Service reported that Yoweri Museveni had warned all foreigners to get out of Uganda to avoid being caught in crossfire. His National Resistance Army was mounting attacks on the main Jinja–Kampala road.

Everyone, including President Obote, knew Museveni would reach Kampala soon. Obote would flee, the army would desert, Museveni would become president. What we didn't know was whether the warning was propaganda.

I warned Schick about this, but he was in no mood to talk with me. On the previous evening when he'd discovered I was in Baker's room he'd tried leading his new crew in some Up-Country

Swahili jokes. *Boy, dry these clothes in the sun, you have broken all the eggs again, just hoe up this grass, you go to the market and buy lamp oil I am going to a meeting of the Europeans . . .* When he wouldn't let go they shifted their interest away from him. Maybe they felt Uganda was more my country than theirs, the British Protectorate thing. They talked to me like I knew something. I was the only one there who'd actually crossed Lake Victoria on a boat and Castro wanted to hear about the steam trains in Tanzania.

So when I warned Schick about Museveni in front of everyone, he had to make face with his compatriots. Normally he'd say something like: blow the fuckers out the way, but this time his face drained and looked like a mechanic's rag.

— Uh, right, does the cunt mean it? What do you guys think?

— Like what's new? Castro said.

— They're nowhere near the Jinja Road, I said. It's propaganda. Anyway, even if it's true, they don't mean today.

He looked at me like I'd called him chicken.

— We'll run it, man, what's the problem. Turnboy! Go warm my seat and scrape the bugs off the windshield . . .

Castro said there'd be a lot of new roadblocks today. Yeah, I said, but you couldn't tell who they were. Schick said:

— If they're all motherfuckers what's it matter who they are?

— If we sit and think about who they are, I said, it would matter.

I thought Schick might be interested in the military picture.

— We'll talk about this in the truck, he said to shut me up.

Castro said that Museveni issued statements like this all the time. He was always telling diplomats, missionaries and foreigners to quit Uganda to prevent 'accidents' happening to them, but they hadn't killed anyone yet. One of the Americans said the Dutch Consulate had just advised its nationals to leave because there'd be another war soon. Castro said he'd heard about some Swiss bloke whose guide murdered him for his Swatch. They found him speared to a tree.

Outside in the truck Schick said:

— We're getting out. We're going to Tanzania. Oogahnda's a bummer, okay?

All Americans pronounced it Oogahnda, the way the British still said Rhodesia and Salisbury.

— Sure, I said, but where yer gonna buy the dope?

— I talked to Castro, the man knows a lot. We're going to Bukoba, on the lake. I aint lettin no kid with a gun get hold of my fuckin truck. Then we just fade into Kenya from there.

— You can't do that, I said. You can't drive round the lake.

— Take the fuckin ferry then, he said.

— With the truck?

— They'll take the truck.

— Did Castro say that?

— He didn't know. He thought so. I dunno.

Let's just figure it out when we get there. All I know is I aint stayin in or coming back through Oogahnda. I'll drive round the friggin lake. There's a road to Kisii.

There were too many gaps in my knowledge here to argue, but I wasn't confident. We should've stayed in Kampala or back-tracked to Jinja. Schick's truck was fine in Kenya where you could buy petrol anywhere. But like a lot of Americans he refused to learn right-hand-drive shift and had got himself an American left-hander, automatic trail-blazer with a power unit under the bonnet that boozed up one gallon every eleven miles. We had to carry eight full jerrycans in the back and a fire extinguisher which might put out a match if we were quick enough. Each jerrycan was padlocked behind a metal bar. In Kampala he was lucky. Castro fixed him up with some gasoline from his vehicle compound, but none of us knew where you got it in Tanzania.

We set off along the Masaka road late morning. Castro called it Hell Road, pounds your shocks to pieces like driving on the moon. At Mpigi roadblock the police were heavily armed and wore shades like they were militia.

— Hey, white men, going to South Africa.

— No, I said. We're going to visit my mother in hospital.

— All white men like to go to South Africa. Take your mother to South Africa or you go in hospital.

— Aw fuck off man, Schick said.

— Why you say that, white monkey?

— He's very sorry, I said. He is trying to stop smoking. It makes him very nervous, you have a gun. Here, take his cigarettes.

I gave him the packet and Schick started revving the engine.

— Go! the policeman shouted. White monkeys!

Schick's idea of supplies had been whisky, beer and tinned chilli beans. It was me who'd gone down the Karen dukas to buy bread, eggs, cooking oil, tea, coffee, Asian home-made crisps, potatoes and rice. We were supposed to have gone north from Kampala, exactly where he hadn't said, except that his 'contact' was selling him four hundred imperial pounds of compressed grass for a hundred dollars. I knew we'd find fruit anywhere, but north of Kampala there might be an old woman selling three onions on a piece of rag or a boy with a paper cornet of groundnuts if you were lucky. Schick said he didn't mind paw-paw but fucked if he was sticking his hands together sucking bluebottles off mangoes. I said if he didn't bring food he'd be on *posho* and *matoke*, but he didn't believe me, he still thought he'd find a tin diner with French fries and six eggs.

Schick's driving was tentative. He'd slow for the potholes or washboards where normally he'd demonstrate the parabolic springs and gas shocks, gunning for that mean speed where the rattling turns to steady hum. Today we rocked and twisted carefully like he'd got a basket of eggs in the back. He was sitting on eggs too, all broody. His stories betrayed anxiety. First he tried getting at me with 'it's you Brits fucked up in Uganda' stuff. Africa was all in the past with us people, he said. Pork skin like Austen still dossin on the doorstep, and look at the goddam Land Rover, he said. Just a World War Two fuckin jeep. Gearbox made of monkey metal, springs like fuckin anvils.

— You Brits have a problem with electrics too. You know we call Mr Lucas 'The Prince of Darkness'. Why do the English drink warm beer? Because Lucas design the refrigeration, hey.

He said he drove a Triumph Spitfire as a kid, thinking it might impress the chicks. He said it would've if Ford had made the gearbox. But American chicks were as bad as British cars. He'd been engaged to one once, back in the States. Marlene. Because he felt sorry for her after smashing her car up. He was driving her home from skiing when a rock fell onto the road and she hyperventilated and wouldn't stop till he said he'd marry her. He thought she was a dork but kinda interesting. She was a bit older than him too. He said women hit their peak aged twenty-seven when they want it seven times a day. Then one day he found out she was a Secret Service wench. She must've been on his case owing to his family all being Green Berets and getting married at Special Forces weddings. She figured he was a security risk, maybe. So one day they went up a mountain to smoke dope and she said she was worried about his driving the car back. Schick had said: what the fuck, I've only had one joint, you could blow me up anytime. That's when he joined the Peace Corps and never went back.

At Mutukula I said he could relax, according to the map we were in Tanzania.

— Look, I said, pointing at a water trough beside the road. That's Tanzanian.

It was a travellers' water trough in the swampy roadside with its flaming torch symbol still intact. It was full of cool rainwater. In the long grass were bits of metal from the tank battles between Tanzania's liberation force and Amin's army. It was a long deserted road, sticky from rain. There was no traffic, no people, no cattle, no roadblocks and Schick flew across the potholes in relief. There were four white flagpoles at the police post but no one in it. Everything was neat and swept. A sign said: *You are now in United Tanzania.* A woman with a mutilated nose was sitting under a tree.

— *Jambo.* Why is no one here? I said.

— It is hatching day. I want *pombe.* You have *pombe?*

— No *pombe.*

For miles along the roadside there were women and children catching termites in net curtains as they hatched. Between the hills we skirted swamp plains till we dropped down into Bukoba. The town had a base camp feel and the buildings looked like East German factories. I could smell the coffee roasting on the heavy air. I asked an old Asian vendor the way to the lake. He sold me five cigarettes and said:

— It is very cold for December, by Jove.

— It's not December, I said. It's April.

— Yes, April by Jove.

At the Flamingo Cafe we ate half-cake with our tea-masala but Schick was restless and wanted to find someone called Shabby, the contact man. I said we should book into the New Bukoba Lodgings first. He said to go back and ask that dog-butt seller if he knew Shabby Shaba the leather-man. India By Jove saw me coming and beckoned me to hurry. He said some special cigarettes had just come in. SM Menthol, twenty shillings. I said the newpapers in Kampala said Bukoba had commodities.

— There are commodities, he said. Much commodoties. Petrol, cooking oil and batteries.

— I want to change money, I said.

— Dollars?

— Maybe. I want to buy leather.

I didn't like this conversation. We were already three steps backwards on this trip and there was nothing worse than travelling south when you want to be north. I wasn't feeling lucky any more.

— You in shoes? he said.

— Yes, I said. Plimsolls. We want to buy shoe leather and take it to Kenya.

— You want elephant hide?

— Yes, I said. To make boots for explorers.

— There is none.

— No one sells leather?

— Yes.

— No or yes?

— No. You want *Wazi-Wazi?*

— What?

— Woman?

— No.

88

— You want man?

— No.

— Boy? Have a boy, please, by Jove, you must enjoy yourself in Bukoba.

— No, thank you, Boy Jove. Where did Amin's areoplanes drop their bombs?

— They bommid the port.

— Where is the port?

— Down there.

— Where's the New Bukoba Lodgings?

— You don't want to stay there.

The wind picked up across the lake, the clouds ran low. The SS *Bukoba* was a three-deck cargo ferry which lilted on its mooring by the harbour wall. It hadn't sailed for three days so there were enough passengers camped out in the grass to sink the thing three times over. No one had tickets yet. The gates were locked and weeds grew along the quayside. Bukoba township was hidden behind outcrops, but the church spire was visible over the banana groves and its bell hung like a bull's testicle. The bell they rang when Amin's Air Force, two meatbox Meteors with one bomb each, came to sink the ferry. They hit a windsock and the rubbish pile and killed a cyclist. I'd seen those Meteors round the back of Entebbe Airport, dumped in the long grass like top-heavy ducks face down in the mud, like the pilots had tried driving them across the fields to escape the Tanzanian *bakombozi* when they came to liberate Kampala.

Schick was hunting his leather merchant down

so the ferry booking fell to me, which meant I had no choice but to sit outside the fence chewing grass like everyone else. A Chinese gunboat chugged out from under the harbour wall and took off in a cloud of spray. A crane loaded coffee into the ferry hold, but not a single cafe in Bukoba had a cup. I walked down to the harbour wall to look at the purple islands ten miles off but the midges drove me back. I asked a man what time the ferry sailed. He said nine o'clock tomorrow night. Third class fifty shillings. The crane started loading bananas and I figured they wouldn't leave bananas in there another twenty-four hours so I asked the man selling groundnuts and cassava cakes when it sailed. Nine o'clock tonight, he said. No, I wasn't about to get on this boat with these people, so I decided to tell Schick we'd have to drive, they weren't taking vehicles.

I'd caught this ferry once before. It was only one day late then but I'd still expected to make the World Service headlines; another overloaded ferry capsized. All on board drowned and eaten by crocodiles. It always sailed at nine in the evening and everyone had to board by sunset or you couldn't see to walk up the gangplank. I'd found a few square feet without bodies on the forward deck against the anchor house. The sky and water were silver and we'd sailed under a dome of cloud dimpled and like the moon hollowed out. The old men talked all night. I fell asleep between bollards and coiled rope thick as legs and dreamt of aeroplane crashes again. It was the eeriest trip I'd ever done and we docked at Mwanza at 5 a.m. to see 26 Class loco steam trains at the railway station, and all the flies which'd sailed with us piled into the New Protein Hotel and landed on the rice and beans and congress tarts.

The Bukoba did capsize in the end. Just about every transport I ever took in Africa came to grief after I'd survived it, aeroplanes included. I took the Flying Crane a couple of times, the Uganda Airlines 707. They used to unbolt the seats and curtain-off the front three-quarters whenever Madame Obote went on shopping trips to London with half a million cash in her handbag. You could look through the curtain and see sports cars roped down and piles of boxes and Harrods bags. One night I dreamt it crashed in Frankfurt. One wet winter evening two weeks later it did.

NINE

At 4 a.m., maybe six hours before the *gendarmes* were due, I put the outside light on. In the sleet Le Haut Bois looked like a *True Detective* murder scene. So, I thought, let's be Nestor Burma, a dirty *flic* revolted by the whole episode. I looked into the core of the dereliction like a dirty copper would and asked out loud: whose gaff is this then? Marcel Macé, *cultivateur.*

I'd spent our first winter at Le Haut Bois wearing Marcel Macé's work trousers round the yard. Blue, pin-striped trousers made of ticking, tied with cord plaited from hemp bailing twine. The last picture ever taken of Marcel shows him wearing these trousers, standing in the Champ-St-Pierre with Juliette, Bijou the Percheron and a visiting couple. The Percheron's head is almost as long as Marcel who shrank over the years. Juliette wears her wooden clogs and her arm's round Marcel's shoulder.

Marcel's Renault 4 saloon was still padlocked inside the garage, a rotten tin-roofed lean-to which hung off the side of the barn. The seats had been gutted by rats, tyres split rotten, electrics chewed, battery foamed, engine and gearbox seized. It had only done seven thousand kilometres. A St Christopher and rosary were hanging from the driver's mirror. The key was rusted in the ignition, a Michelin man on the fob with a metal dog-tag Marcel must have made himself, punching out his name, Marcel Macé, *cultivateur*. His wallet was still in the glove box. Fifty francs, his voting card, hunting permit, driver's licence, and his last hospital appointment with a doctor's prescription. He'd parked the car there over twenty years back, locked the garage, then died at home three weeks later.

There was no point trying to sleep. I switched the World Service on and kept vigil till sunrise. By now the books which sprawled down the front steps and into the mud were so wet they flopped to pieces when I picked them up. The fragments of Joy among the refuse angered me because I didn't want to remember her right then. I didn't want her in on this. I'd done the crime, so I'd do the investigating. But seeing her trinket box, discarded and crushed, made me feel like the hired killer who'd dumped Joy under the floorboards with a broken neck. I invented her last thoughts, maybe she whispered them. *You didn't have to do it, we could've talked . . .* Sure, we could've but we didn't. I didn't want to know. I was there to pick at time, just the archaeology of marriage. The top layer didn't matter, it was already smashed through, that concrete which had sealed all truth. You just come across the trinkets and broken pots. I was looking for the strata where love became extinct and you can break into your own derelict house just to wreck it. Only someone had got there first. So what had gone wrong here?

I'd never told Yannick I wanted the place

trashed. I just wanted the insurance money. I *needed* the insurance money, because when Joy left, her father's meagre allowance left with her. I'd given Yannick specific instructions to make it an authentic break-in. Everything I didn't want stolen would be locked in the barn, except the Calvados and the big oak marriage chest. They could take anything else and sell it. They could strew a reasonable mess. I'd let Yannick off the money he owed me. I'd cover any tyre tracks by driving or walking all over them. I'd give him first refusal on anything in the barns. If I got a big payback off the insurance I'd chuck in a *pourboire* for the burglers. So what was this violent, mean shit all about?

I made my statement to the gendarmes later that morning, a *Dépot de Plainte contre un auteur inconnu*, a complaint against an unknown author. Numb from lack of sleep, I had bruisy rings under bloodshot eyes, a case-book victim face. The chaotic state of the place distracted them in any case. The head *pandore* filled the forms in, checking the time on his square watch. 11 a.m. I made a list of the missing articles and we stabbed at meanings and descriptions and values. We put a few sleet-sodden dictionaries on the nearest barrel because they insisted I bring them in now, there was no need to have taken them so literally and left them out all night. The *pandore* sat cross-legged and I was sure he'd got women's tights on under his blue trousers which sounded like a skirt when his flabby legs brushed together. His squeaky voice had no volume and piped out through pursed lips, like a plastic trumpet or a little fat boy blowing out his first smoke from a rolled-up sheet of exercise book. His cardboard cap was on a chair.

There's something bullet-proof about a foreign language. My struggle to construct simple sentences became that blank, numb shame of a victim of crime and desertion. Speaking French so badly meant I couldn't've given myself away if I tried. But then I couldn't pick up any sensitivity in the *pandores* either. It seemed to me they were looking for clues on how I managed to live in this hovel, trying to clear away the mess and damage in their minds, wondering if what was left, what the burglars saw when they'd entered, was a normal household they wouldn't feel obliged to smash up, even within the rugged perimeters of life in the bocage.

— *Où est votre femme?* he said.

Words, like handcuffs, whipped out from behind his back.

— *En Afrique*, I said, seizing an opportunity to rehearse my lines for the next hundred performances. *Son père est mort.*

The trainee *flic* took a photo of the floor where the bench had been, getting his boots in the way. Then he looked at the glasses on the chair, pointing out the fingerprints. There shouldn't have been any fingerprints, but they could've been mine, or even Joy's. The *pandore* hesitated, then said he wanted my fingerprints and the assistant *flic* lifted the kit from the crime case.

— Where exactly is your wife? Her address?

— I don't know, I said.

The day after she'd left an envelope arrived in the post, a white file card inside with one solitary line: *Gone to Africa, can't come back.* I couldn't show anyone that. Her name wasn't even on it, like she hadn't decided yet what her new name would be. She must've written the card at Le Haut Bois, changing the words in her head from command: *Go to Africa, don't come back,* to fait accompli. It had the Briouze postmark too, so she must've posted it at the railway station, under my nose, behind my back. The head *pandore* rolled my fingers on the ink pad then rolled them on the fingerprint sheet. I washed off the ink under an ice cold tap, then it took even longer to fumble in the dictionary every time I needed a word. At one point I wanted to say: they even took the condoms. And the word, the fucking word I used was *prophylactics*, the same word you use in East Africa for malaria pills. Something I hadn't thought of struck me: had Joy been taking malaria tablets for three weeks in secret? What about her jabs? Had I noticed any swellings, any fever? Could she really just get on a plane to Africa two days after deciding to go?

— Your wife, she comes back when? the *pandore* said.

— Don't know, I said.

— Where is she?

— Africa.

— No no, you give us her address, okay?

After they'd gone it was time to note details and settle some of the disquiet, climb down before I fell.

One thing was certain. They hadn't turned into the yard because there'd been no tracks in the mud. So whoever they were, they hadn't trusted me to cover them. They'd either backed down the *chemin* or backed up it. To get in the house they'd smashed a low corner pane of the back window, but on the wrong side of the catch. Probably startled by the noise it made, they didn't smash another, just came round the front, smashed a pane there and climbed into the study, knocking the little souvenir bell off the sill. It wasn't on the floor and I couldn't find it in the house, so the monkey must've pocketed it, attracted by the tinkling or the bronze shine. This set the pattern for his behaviour. A magpie burglar, a blagger's apprentice who didn't play for the team. The bell was worthless for chrissake, a commemorative ornament to mark the casting of a new bell for the church at St-André-de-Briouze, a bell called Catherine. Everyone in the *commune* was given one, cast from the old bell which they'd melted down. The Curé had driven round and handed one to all his parishioners with a blessing, the only thing to make us feel we belonged there.

From here our bellboy must've been sent to the desk to look for the keys. He found the barn key and, by some miracle, it fitted the lock of the house door, but only from the inside. I didn't know that. Brains was let in, he was the *brocanteur*, or at least the more experienced. Bellboy was sent upstairs where he piled things at random into the camping fridge. He thought he'd found the jewellery box only it was all Juliette Macé's cheap *cult catholique*.

97

He snapped the rosaries and flung the beads all over the floor then grabbed a shirt and began to wipe his fingerprints off the box. He took an African wallet and eighteen English Durex Gossamer which Joy had got free at the Family Planning years back. He humped the fridge downstairs and out on to the steps. Meanwhile Brains had taken everything he considered valuable into the light and accidently knocked all the glass off the desk. He opened some booze, poured out two glasses and told the bell-boy to start taking his selection outside, table first. This proved his pedigree. I didn't know it at the time, but the table was worth *une brique*, a grand. Then out went the olive bench, some trinkets and the Sabatier knives, but just the stabbing sizes. A dwindling list after that, a growing urgency or dis-appointment. Cassette radio with a broken aerial and a Bach tape still in it. Boots binoculars. Pair of rub-bish cufflinks. Something must've disturbed them, or it wasn't worth the risk now they were considering cutlery and Swahili–English dictionaries. At some point they'd found the Calvados and rejoiced at that, taking all the bottles with the black string tied round the neck. They left the most valuable item, the 500-year-old marriage chest, but took the crappy phone that cost me twenty francs at a *vide-grenier*. Then they abandoned the house, leaving the books and fridge on the steps and everything else scattered over the floor.

I was interrupted by Aunay standing in the doorway shouting: *où sont mes bêtes?* Red wine nose, clogs, work trousers, no cap, rain clinging to his face, hands like boxing gloves holding two little red flags. His voice was slipping, he looked defeated and helpless and for a moment I felt this flicker of pity. He'd caught me sweeping up the glass and shuffling Juliette's papers back into bin-bags, all those bundles of unburned necrology from 1901, brown paper packets bursting with black-edged funeral notices. Fat little Marcel Macé lookalikes in Renault 4s still delivered them to Le Haut Bois when someone in the *commune* died, like the place was on the infinite rota of death. There were dozens for Marcel's funeral, new and still in the printer's packet. It was these I had in my hand now.

Pierre Aunay stood there like he'd stumbled in on their deaths all over again. Or perhaps he thought his beasts had broken in and smashed the place up. For a second I wondered that myself. His beasts trampled through fences weekly, horning the rickety old posts till they snapped at the root. The whole *troupeau* would nudge cautiously down to my yard, sampling the verge or making a hop for it up the lane and into the road. Prodhomme would have to round them up and herd them into the nearest field. Aunay lived twenty kilometres away on his rundown farm without a phone, so you had to ring the callbox in his village and let it ring for two days till someone answered, usually some fuckin salesman who'd slam the phone down saying no he would not go to some *plouc*'s farm to tell him his beasts had escaped. It took up to four days for Aunay to turn up with his little red flags and wheyyyy-eyyyyy the beasts back down the lane. When he found the breach he darned it with bale twine or banged in a new splint.

Aunay had worked for the Macés after the war as herdsman, so how many times had he bodged these fences? Back then he'd lived in one of the two ruins at the top of the track. When Marcel died, Juliette had sold Aunay eleven hectares for a sous, perhaps from loyalty, or maybe Aunay just banged on the widow's door in the rain one day and asked for it. Prodhomme said that when Juliette finally abandoned Le Haut Bois, Aunay spent nights in the barns.

The land was no *cadeau* anyway, just a network of tiny acidic fields, bogged and spoilt by great tangles of bramble thicket, tick-infested fern and termite stumps. Some was classified as just ground, the rest meadow, the remains of pear orchards, old trees split and deformed, apple trees strangled in mistletoe, a derelict stable made of mud, a cowshed with broken windows. Prodhomme rented him a few adjoining fields, but he never paid the rent. It was only eighty francs a year and a side of beef.

Aunay didn't drive. He still moved his beef with horse and cart and kept the rain off with a fertiliser bag tied round his waist. He'd gone bankrupt twice, his land seized by bailiffs and auctioned by candle, where the buyer was the highest bidder at the extinction of the candle flame. No one bid so he transferred the land into his wife's name and nothing at Le Haut Bois changed.

Aunay clobbed off down the mudslide before I had a chance to open my mouth anyway, just shaking his head going *ooooorrrrrrrrrrr*. I wasn't after respect from this man, but I couldn't believe he'd had any for Juliette Macé either. The state she kept the place in must've perplexed him, even angered him. And all that equipment Aunay could never afford just left to disintegrate in the sheds. She never let him have so much as a rusty horseshoe. And Le Haut Bois had been a wealthy farm once. There was a baronial fireplace and an Anglo-Norman archway in the big stone barn. I'd found all the account books and diaries going back to 1817. Juliette cramped her war-time figures into a half-filled diary begun by Madame Lecoeur in 1896. Between old accounts of the sale to Geo Baptiste of eggs, cider, coffee and salted pork, Juliette listed produce she'd sold to black marketeers who'd walked across the fields at night in 1942. Hams, butter, cheese, cream, eggs and ducks which went to Paris in women's suitcases or wrapped in brown paper and string by parcel van from the Gare de Briouze. Dairy cream for expectant mothers, ox-tongue for the doctor. So whose hank of blonde hair was it I'd found hidden on the ridge beam in the *grenier*? An entire woman's plait hacked through, with a German dictionary beside it. Had Juliette been betrayed? Had Juliette gone round the *commune* shaving off the hair of collaborators, the women Madame Cardonel had told us 'knitted' with the Germans? I liked to think that Juliette had been betrayed and had kept this token of revenge.

101

TEN

The wind dropped as the sun set so I began the four-kilometre walk back to Bukoba township. We'd booked into the New Bukoba Lodgings but I figured Schick was in some bar. I gave up after the first two, they were full of *Wazi-Wazi* who wanted me to buy them beer. One of them followed me back from the Moonlight Bar to the New Bukoba, a little Chagga girl who couldn't've been eighteen. She kept trying to paddle her fingers on my palm. She wore white trousers and a tight woolly jumper. Her hair was long, looped and beaded.

— I don't have money, I said.

— Buy me one beer, she said.

In the compound the tables were filling up and a band was unloading equipment. Jamil Music Taarab. I was hungry but the food was in the truck and the truck was wherever Schick was. I did have my own money but beans and rice was seventy-five shillings. The official rate was fourteen shillings to one pound sterling.

— How much is beer? I said.

— Hundred, the Chagga said.

— No!

— Yes.

— I must eat food.

— I wait, she said.

I tried nine cafes. Six had boiled eggs and tea-masala, four had juice and rice cakes. I decided to wait for Schick. The Indian 'Boy Jove' was outside the Lake Eating Happy Cafe but his cigarettes were finished.

— Only *njugu*. You want *njugu?*

— No.

— You want whisky for your girl?

— What girl?

— Nema. The Chagga. Very bad girl.

— Is she *Wazi-Wazi?*

— No, by Jove. *Malaya fundi.* Very experience. She not speak Swahili. The Greek man bring the Chagga here. She let the baby die and he beat her, oh, very terribly by Jove. She throw the baby in a toilet and the police come and ask with whom is this baby. No one tell them because the Greek man, he is in business and pay tea money to everyone.

I was still wondering if Schick's leather-man Shabby was real.

— Is he in leather?

— There is no leather.

— Is his name Shabby?

— No. Ask your friend.

— Nema?

— No, the one you are with. He is there.

— You mean Schick, the American? In the jeep?

— Yes yes.

— Okay, I buy *njugu*.

So Schick had lied about Shabby, that was his bent coat-hanger method of keeping me guessing.

103

He didn't want me around at the deal, but that was understandable. If there was no Shabby, there was just a Greek importer with a Chagga girl he'd told to get lost while he did business with Schick. I thought I knew where I stood then.

Back at the New Bukoba, Jamil Music Taarab were scraping the oven out. No one clapped between songs, they just went on shouting to each other as beer bottle tops hit the concrete. A waiter was serving something hot so I went to examine the kitchen vats. Propped on the counter was a black-board and chalk menu. Beef curry. I found a table in the corner of the compound. Nema slipped on to a chair beside me and sat with her hands folded over her crotch.

— Buy me one beer. Please.

I was watching for headlights, but I knew Schick wouldn't show that night. He was simply drinking the Greek man's beer, sampling his porn and getting stoned. That was okay by me. I didn't want to watch him bite beer bottles in half at my table then buy a few slaps off Nema, or just drag her through his door saying her sugar daddy was paying. So I shouted for a beer, and even more irrationally shouted for a Johnnie Walker which I didn't want but thought I needed. The waiter left five shillings change which Nema slipped into her back pocket.

— We go disco? she said.

— This disco?

— No, where I coming from. In Dar'Salaam. Me very bad, you very bad.

The beer cost twenty shillings, the Johnnie

Walker seventy bloody five. The hair and the fly were free, or it was a cocktail, Fly Catcher. Like Venus next to me who'd shoved up an inch and leant her knee against my leg, sucking on her bottle.

— Where do you live? I said.

— Outside. She pointed vaguely towards the lake.

— With the Greek?

— Ach. Grik very bad man. You very good boy.

— What's his name, the Grik?

— *Mafuta Mingi.*

I laughed, and she laughed at me. *Mafuta Mingi* meant loads of fat, oil, petrol. Not a nice term for rich men, but a prostitute's one.

— He is with *mzungu?* American?

— Yes, he say me: go away, I do business. Merican bad man too?

— Yes, I said. Very bad.

— You go Dar'Salaam tomorrow? You tek me.

She put a hand on my thigh now and rubbed it like I'd got hyperthermia.

— One beer, she said. There is no more. We go your room now?

I didn't know.

— Is no problem, she said.

But it was a problem. She was a comfort girl and I felt like Schick junior. I realised I just made bad copies of the person I happened to be with. My search for personality had fallen on a barren ego. I never knew what to say, so conversation was like Scrabble. I felt I had to get over Joy before I'd even met her, with the help of this semi-literate Chagga

105

girl who was offering simple, uncoded comfort. We knew twenty words between us but they were suddenly the best twenty words I'd spoken in years.

My room was off the courtyard, half-cage, half-cell. Foam mattress, pink sheet and a dim electric bulb that worked. The fan rotated below the bulb so the light had to fire through the propellers like an old bi-plane fighter. Nema sat on the bed and took off her jumper. Underneath, she wore a black sling-back T-shirt.

— Five hundred shilling I stay night.

— I don't have five hundred shilling.

Suddenly our twenty words became corrupted. I didn't want to give her money for this, not now. I needed every shilling I had in any case.

— Three hundred shilling, she said.

— I don't have three hundred shilling.

— Two hundred shilling, for fuck. I stay. Yes? Please.

— I don't have.

— Is true? You don't have one hundred?

— No.

She stood up, sat down. Put her jumper back on.

— Is true? she said again.

It struck me how little I really did have. I did some hasty reckoning.

— Is true, I said. I have to sell clothes.

— What cloth-ies?

I rifled through my rucksack and took out my raincoat, a white shirt, and a red T-shirt.

— These. I sell these. And this.

I added a battery-powered electric razor I'd bought for shaving in droughts. It was sure to rain soon so I could use my Flying Sun Chinese blades now.

— And my watch, I said, adding it to the pile.

She tried on my raincoat and the shirt, throwing them back on the bed.

— No good. Vey bad. I get you money.

She opened the door.

— You come back? I said, sounding so unlike myself.

— Yes, she said. I get you thousand shillings.

— Just come back, I said.

Two hours of rain banged on the tin roof that night but I left my door unlocked and slept with everything in the bed with me. I didn't hear Schick's truck and I woke alone. It was a Saturday morning. In the kitchen a man in a yellow hat, blue coat and green shirt was chopping up a goat under the fan. There was boiled eggs and coffee. A boy was sweeping the bottle tops and fag ends round the tables outside. He looked sharp so I told him I had things to sell and we went and looked at them set out on the bed. He was disappointed, even after I added a blank tape, but he tried on the raincoat greedily enough.

— You give me, you help me as friend, to remember. My name they is calling me is Gosto sir.

— The price is five hundred shillings, I said. Tape fifty shillings. Battery *wembe* one thousand shillings. Watch one thousand. Shirt one hundred. T-shirt fifty. Yes? You know where to sell?

— Yes. I am coming, I will get your price.

— When?

— Eleven o'clock.

My prices were absurdly high, I would never get them. Gosto would probably come back with a five-bob note. A loudspeaker relayed Tanzanian radio into the compound. The programme began with a gong and five people walked into the yard from the bar like they'd been summoned. Then trumpets and two more people stood by the loud-speaker. A Volvo drew up and some real *mafuta mingi* got out dripping in watches and chains, the women in high heels, jeans and little red handbags. They called for meat and the women smoked like flappers. The knot of listeners gathered round the loudspeaker were enthralled by the news. One of them pointed at me. Gosto was there with his broom so I assumed he'd mentioned I was holding a bedtop sale. I wondered if Boy Jove would make a better agent than Gosto. I found him sitting on a wooden parlour chair outside his premises, smoking his pipe in a brown suit and floppy cricket hat, listening to the radio.

— By Jove, my friend, there is trouble, eh? Why did she do it? You are lucky to be free man by Jove?

I realised 'by Jove' was an expression of gravity. His pipe was swaying like a censer.

— What trouble? I said, my optimism gone.

— The news, by Jove, is broadcast on the redio. That girl, your girl, oh, *malaya fundi*, now she is in the high jump. She killed him, by Jove they say she killed him for five hundred shillings.

— Killed who?

108

— The redio say one Greek and one Italian.

— The Chagga? Nema? What Italian?

I knew this wasn't the usual tricky nonsense. They must've meant Schick, unless Boy Jove had got it wrong. I couldn't even remember Schick's surname. I'd only seen it written down once, in a hotel register. It hadn't looked Italian; Stalsen, Statten, Stutter, something like that. No fuckin 'o' on the end. It certainly wasn't obvious like Rich Pagano or Schick Stiletto.

— You didn't see the detectives? Boy Jove said.

— No, where?

— I don't know where. There is investigation by Jove. The CID.

This gave me some respite. It could all be a hoax after all.

— When did she kill these men?

— In the night, by Jove. After you made with her.

— I didn't . . . when was it on the radio?

— The bulletin. Just half-one hour. Oh by Jove, another calamity in Bukoba. My friend, you must quickly secure the means.

Gosto knocked on my door as I was packing. He said he'd found a man to buy the battery *wembe*.

— Give me coat for two hundred shillings.

— Okay, here.

He was amazed, or he knew they were coming for me. The man wanted to see the shaver so I gave it to Gosto to show him.

— There is policey-man waiting you, he said,

and went. I packed and went outside, leaving my rucksack under the bed.

The policeman was sitting at a table in a pea-green woman's raincoat with big glass buttons. He was drunk, propping his chin with his hand, breathing heavily. Several people sat at the table and the *mafuta mingi* turned to watch from a few yards away. I was told to sit. The manager said this was Kianjiji, CID.

— Show me your warrant card.

— Ach, he said, banging his hand on the table so the flies jumped.

— Identity, I said.

— You, for you, he said, problem money, for me problem money. This girl, you sleep with *jana*, very bad she, ah, shooting, for five hundred shillings, now murder case. For you, problem money suspected person *wewe*, for you, prison, me to prison tomorrow, you with her to killing with money . . .

Seemed like an open and shut case to me. Just find the missing word.

— I want interpreter, I said.

— You shoosh!

Gosto was showing the *mafuta mingi* the shaver. The man clicked it on, put it to his face and gave himself a shave over his meat. His girl laughed. He pretended to shave his teeth and the back of her hand.

— You, prison, shooting case, he started up again. You pray *mungu*, no helping, killing with money is for me bail five hundred shillings.

It started raining, two or three clouts on the table

then a cloudburst. We all ran inside. Kianjiji CID was last in and got soaked. He started looking round for me.

— Shooting case is prison. Witness now, you boy! *Njoo!*

Gosto put the shaver in his trouser pocket but it stuck out through a rip. Kianjiji started shouting in Swahili and the *mafuta mingi* tutted and said something. I asked Kijama the cook what was happening.

— He want evidence from Gosto.

— What evidence?

— I do not know.

— YOU MZUNGU SHOOSH!

— I want a lawyer.

— You money in station, you prison case. Chagga prison with murder, you prison with shooting money.

— I want to telephone the British High Commission.

— You station charge, *wewe*, bail, five hundred dollar.

Everyone was shouting now and making hand signals and Kianjiji sat there shaking his head as a big trail of snot detached itself and stuck to his collar. He stood up.

— I go warrant, I come custody, eleven o'clock, Nema stateyment all case, shooting, money, prison, whole case problem money *wewe* . . .

He walked off like a man with blisters in his tennis shoes. His incoherence had scared me though, and everyone else looked worried too. The *mafuta mingi* asked me how much I wanted for the shaver.

111

I'd forgotten and said five hundred shillings. Gosto looked disappointed when I accepted. The *mafuta mingi* asked me if I played draughts. A man came in with a red suitcase and dropped his bottle of *konyagi* on the floor. Everyone's interest shifted as he tried several ways of scooping it up. The cook got him a cup. Two chickens tried to peck it. Gosto tried it on with me:

— My friend, come here and give me five shillings.

— I gave you my coat, I said.

— But you have much trouble. You must run away.

— Sell my watch and I give you five shillings.

The cook swiped Gosto round the head with his hand which still had meat blood on it.

— Is it true? I asked the cook. The girl. She killed these people?

— It was said on the news bulletin, one Greek, one Italy. It might be lies.

— What do I do? Is he coming back, the CID?

— Yes. He wants money. He make trouble for you. You must go quickly. Where is your friend?

— I don't know.

— You must pay me ninety shillings and go.

ELEVEN

When the *gendarmes* came back next day I was on my knees with all the photographs I could find of Juliette, in chronological order. I scooped them up like I was a card sharp and slipped them under the armchair. I don't know why, like the way I used to pull down my Frida Kahlo posters in London if certain people rang the doorbell. The head *pandore* rubbed his hands in the cold and kept his *kepi* on his head.

Their photos hadn't come out well and they wanted to take more, starting with the glasses, but the camera in their crime case was a pocket automatic with a built-in flash, so the fingerprints would never show up anyway. Luckily for him I hadn't washed the glasses, so he took them outside into the daylight and the drizzle. This was one of the most depressing moments of my life, not entirely for its present state but its reflexive backwardness. The dead light, the images still in my eyes of the photos of widow Juliette camped in her filth, the dampness on our clothes from the drizzle, the dirty cracked coffee cups and the grouty, plughole coffee going cold beside the powdered glasses. The *pandore* took his wonky pictures of the broken window too and the bits of smashed tumbler still left on a muddy carpet. I

113

suppose it just triggered leakage of the past like rain through the broken window.

He took more blurred close-ups of my draining board, a jag of dirty glass, wet dictionaries we'd put back outside so they appeared to tumble down the granite steps in the rain like the day before.

The *flic* would say: where was the clock? I'd point. He'd walk back and forth and flick his little switch on the camera function dial from the picture of a tree to the picture of a face. Focus, flashette. *Voila*, French surrealism too, a shadow in the dust on a dirty bit of desktop, dead rose and dried up bit of snakeskin poking out the corner.

I tried to explain my deductions of the previous day, but the head *pandore* thought little of them. He just threw up his hands and asked if I knew Yannick Thiboult. I was ready for that one. I said yes, he owed me money. Was it him? I asked so innocently. No, he said, this was the work of *voyageurs*. Or perhaps I'd seen an Arab loitering in the lane, *oui?*

Why would an Arab want broken drill bits, snapped plastic gutter fixtures, a bag of rusty staples and snapped ruler and a clapped-out non-retrieving tape measure? Yes yes yes, but they had an idea. They weren't interested in looking at the evidence. Yoohoodi and Zeep did this job, he said. Two *crapules Arabes*.

A week later I was looking through *L'Orne Combattante* to see if the break-in was on the *Fait Divers* page. I thought it might say if the police arrested any *crapules* too. But what do I see but a photograph of my *pandore* X. His boss was leaving. *Depart du commandant de gendarmerie. Amitié, solidarité et réalité du metier.* Like an apple bobbing on a muddy pond, there was his face among the *pandores*, all looking like winners in a draw for the mountain bike. And fuck me there he was again, in this picture of a group of *colombophiles*, out of the rain with his tie still straight, smiling on his pals who take stock of the year's activity over a glass of friendship during some amicable hours. In the photograph they hand the medal to L. Houdini whose pigeon flew 590 kilometres *par un vent de sud-ouest* from Bayonne last July.

Me and Joy had been in the local paper, photographed on the edge of some event like the Foire de Sainte-Catherine in Briouze, our two blurred heads near the *pissoir*. You could see it was us in our L. L. Bean caps and my copious yak wool jumper. It was late November, our first winter in France, and we'd knocked off early to go mingle at the Foire. It was a Norman tradition, the day to buy and plant fruit trees as Sainte Catherine made sure they took root.

Everything fascinated us, even if the Foire was nothing extraordinary, just a row of tractors by the bank, a nurseryman selling saplings, a horsemeat butcher, fruit and veg stalls, the girdle and housecoat van, the chainsaw shop and *Monsieur Gros Pneus*, Big Tyres. We were photographed looking at two rows of young beasts roped to the galvanised barriers. Aunay was there too with all the stunted old farmers in their best caps and baggy jackets, beating their sitting calves back upright with hazel poles. We were

115

baffled by the fury of the beating but it doesn't show on our faces. In the photo we were too far away, like it was a 4D time picture, two accidental particles wandered in from the future.

Juliette had kept her cuttings too. At the Foire de Sainte-Catherine in 1980, Madame the widow Macé, Juliette, of Le Haut Bois, St-André-de-Briouze was photographed by *L'Orne Combattante* on the Monday evening at the prize-giving ceremony, receiving her FM battery-powered transistor radio. A whole third of her face hangs below her mouth. She's standing in the electrical shop with four other winners, wearing her navy blue coat with the big buttons. Three winners have the radio in its box, the other two show it off. Juliette never did get hers out the box and she was too mean to give it away. I'd found it where she threw it, the earplug socket rusted up and the battery inside corroded. I'd found the blue coat too, chewed by rats and thrown up the stairway to the loft, along with her shoes and walking canes and handbags and sardine tins. The cutting from the paper was in the medicine cabinet with the last twenty years of doctor's receipts and Marcel's hunting permits.

I pulled up outside L'Atelier de Merlin, the old primary school at Ste-Honorine, looking for Yannick. Gilles was sitting on the pavement outside, back against the wall, wearing his leather trousers, earrings like tea-towel holders and a pirate's head scarf. He was juggling oranges and skittles. In the corridor, another *mec* had tied his bull Staff to a table leg and was playing patience, some warped Johnny Halliday vinyl on an old record player on the floor by the back door. Yannick was sitting in the sticky, yellow kitchen. The scalloped lead ashtrays were full and bottles of liqueurs with bar spouts covered the table. It was 10.30 a.m. At the kitchen sink this *pute* with dry black hair and peeling lips tried washing up a stack of plates without breaking her nails or getting the cigarette too wet to suck, while Yannick was blowing on his fingerless mitt ends. One of his nails was blackened and the thread looped off the cuffs of his acrylic cardigan. There were bags and heaps of clothes in the yard, some under shelter, some strewn by the dog over what was once the playground. I realised he must've hunted through these bags once a week, worn what fitted till it stank before throwing it on the heap. The same with his dishes, pots and cutlery. If he threw a grease-clagged frying pan across the yard, the dog would lick it clean and some Parisian would pay twenty francs for it.

His albino dog had nine puppies and there were dog *crottes* in every room, old and new, trails of them in the playground, on the clothes, the rusty metal, in the sinks lined along the ground by the fence, and even on top of a rusty old stove by the gate. He didn't attempt to smile, just said he'd have my money by August.

— I don't understand, I said. We had business, no?

— The *flics* came here, he said.

I didn't know the French for 'so what'.

— *Oui?* I said, shrugging the shoulders so it

meant the same thing. The police were always clocking him. I found out why from someone I knew in Flers whose old man was an ex-policeman who'd retired to a little house in Ste-Honorine and got himself elected to the village council. The council had wanted to rent the disused primary school out to an artisan, or an *enterprise*. The classroom would be a workshop, the playground for materials, the living quarters upstairs. Yannick applied as a furniture restorer/*brocanteur*. The council met to discuss the application. Only the retired *flic* objected. On a majority vote Yannick moved in for a nominal rent. The *flic* paid him an early visit and threatened to burn the place down with Yannick and his rubbish inside. He said he'd be watching Yannick every day and he'd make sure the police stopped him every time he got into his van. He said if ever he met him outside on his own in the dark he'd smash his teeth in.

The police were always checking the serial numbers in Yannick's books against the rubbish in his yard and the dismantled oak *armoires* in his workshop. They never found anything, so they'd frisk Gilles and do the vehicles. Spot fines for a bald spare, hole in the exhaust, faulty headlamp. They stopped Yannick's van whenever they saw it. On the way back from *vide greniers*, in the carpark, at the church. They breathalised him, even did Gilles for not wearing a seat belt in the passenger seat as they pulled away from the *boulangerie*.

— They wanted what? I said.
— *Camelote*, he said.

118

I still didn't understand his problem. We both knew they'd come looking routinely. We moved into the yard and walked hands in pockets toward a white diesel *cuisinière*. Some English ice-cream man living in Segrie had told me it was sitting in the playground. It was a John Lee stove, only worth a hundred francs but it ran on pink diesel which was only 13p a litre. I could even run the Land Rover on that, the police would never know. I was desperate to find a cheap form of heat now I'd run out of wood, and the daily scavenge was taking me wider and wider, making the wheelbarrow impractical, and the dragging of slimey, frozen trunks impossible. I'd always been warmed more by the recuperation and the cutting than the burning. The Normans said the best firewood warmed you three times: gathering, cutting, burning. The stove was over by the fence and Yannick followed me like he was on a piece of string.

— Yes, I said. My *camelote*.

— I don't have it, he said.

I lifted the enamel cover. The cast-iron top was pitted with new rust. I lifted the hot-plate ring and peered at the black plaque, diesel fur and the oily orange soot.

— It works, Yannick said. Two hundred francs.

— My *camelote*, I know, I said. Your friends took it. It's far, I hope.

— No, they didn't take it.

— They did.

— No, he said.

— Someone did, I said. Left the place like a

119

bordello. Terrible uhm *bordello*, broken glass everywhere, my good things taken . . .

Maybe they'd told Yannick they hadn't done it. Maybe he was lying. He didn't look like a good liar, but now he looked like he'd do anything for two hundred francs. When he'd first owed us money we'd go there and pick out a book or an old coffee pot from his stock and he'd say take it, *cadeau*. But after the woman and three kids moved in he'd accept a franc because they cut his phone off and he had to use the coin box the other side of the road. But now he denied that Gilles and the bellboy blagged the place he didn't have to stick to his agreement and could ask two hundred francs for the John Lee stove.

— Who did that thing? I said. It's not coincidence.

Yannick shrugged his bony shoulders. One shrug and he almost dislocated his arm. He looked shorter than before. His damp shoe-ettes squelched and he looked at the ground, at glass stalagtites from a chandelier, ceramic cider bottle tops, a plastic framed Mother of God with gilt highlights just like Juliette's. Over by the fence about a dozen sheep snicked among the worm casts and mole hills in the field. On the pavement was a disused weighbridge. Along the fence, a line of old wash basins, pissoirs, bidets and shower trays which must've come from some hotel. There was a sit-up-and-beg bath on three legs. I walked over to it, Yannick rocked forward, came halfway and stopped.

— How much? I said.

He came the rest of the way reluctantly just so

I'd notice he wasn't going to follow me around the yard any more. He ran his finger round the tap hole on top and took some grime away, like now it was re-conditioned and he could raise the price.

— Fifty francs.

— One hunded and fifty the two, I said pointing to the *cuisinière*.

This time his shrug was pitiable. He said he couldn't deliver them because they'd taken the van back and scrapped it. He'd had to borrow the blue Deux Chevaux parked outside.

— You have my money in August?

He said perhaps. He said there were too many *camelotes* in Flers now. It was hard.

— The bank? I said.

He shook his head. One thing I'd never understood was how come Yannick got himself voted on to the village council with that ex-*flic*, unless there were only seven men who could read in the whole village. Every week in the *L'Orne Combattante* for as long as I could remember, that is if the little box reserved for Ste-Honorine had any news in it at all, Yannick Thiboult was always listed 'absent without notice' from the council meetings.

My next visitors at Le Haut Bois were the insurance broker and the *Ingenieur-expert* who'd been employed by the insurance company to expose fraud or prove the non-liability of my claim. They drove in like a car advert, two clean slim men about my age, over-scented and shaved smooth to the bone, cling-film faces, poncy and contemptuous.

I had stove pipes all over the steps and on the path, hacksaw screeching in my ear as I cut, bent, and measured out the right lengths. Diesel snow swirled about in the wind. As they walked up to me the agent said to the *expert*:

— He doesn't speak French. Talk with Madame.

— Madame's not here, I said.

They saw my hands were black and withdrew their offer to shake. Not that I'd offered anyway; these people had come to prove me a liar. Nine hundred francs a year we'd paid them.

The investigator didn't believe me, I could see that. A freelance called out from Caen, the man with a suitcase. He walked in the house and pulled out the plug from the electric drill I was using to buff the iron plates on the stove. Just pulled it out and threw it on the ground. He spent the next hour trying to invalidate the insurance cover by insisting the house wasn't fit or habitable to be a *residence principale*. If he could prove it was a second home my claim was fraudulant.

— How can you live with this cold? he said.

He put his hand on all the drafts, shook his head, took photographs of each window and said:

— What sort of house is it? You don't have the *cuisinière* near the *point d'eau* and there's no insulation or heating or sanitation. You really live here?

At one point he went out back to photograph the broken window and a goose came round the corner after him, making the bastard slip over and cut his hand on a piece of glass. He came in dabbing the cut with a handkerchief and brushing the wet

122

mud off his knee. The broker tried to reassure me. I said all old *fermettes* had the stove in the chimney and the water down the other end. It was Juliette Macé . . . Yes, yes, he said, don't worry, he knew we lived there, but there might be a problem if we'd been absent for more than ninety days between premiums.

— You er go in England, er for live er isn't you? he said in worse English than my French.

— *Non, jamais*, I said. Fuck him.

— Okay okay, he said. He wanted to call in the week to verify my list of stolen items and their value. He said I needed the receipts or some proof of ownership and purchase.

The two of them stood conferring down by the lane, hunched in the cold, one eye each on the mud in case it jumped them. The *expert* tapped his pen a few times on his folder, the broker kept his hands tight in bottle-green slacks, his black document case pinched tight under his wing. They shook hands, the *expert* driving away first. It was dark. I rounded up the animals, wedged the barn door shut and put the stove together.

TWELVE

I fled Bukoba before Kianjiji CID came back for his shooting money, and headed back to Uganda. Two men in Kampala bus park said Obote got so drunk in public now he wet his trousers.

— I have to go north, I said. Is there transport?

— The pipple are even frightened to travel to Jinja. You must take the train because it is protected, by the soldiers, haha, oh my friend, these ones shoot at some banana trees!

The other man said he was in a car just the day before when an Acholi soldier stopped it with his rifle and forced them to go the other way. The soldier saw a man with a fish and ordered the man to put the fish in the boot. Then he bought *wargi* and demanded to have the fish roasted. When the soldier was drunk he said it was because he'd had a bad day. They'd gone on the rampage and killed nine people in Mukono, outside Kampala. The man asked why. The soldier said: well, they complained about our roadblock.

— These Acholi sodjer are killing Buganda pipple isn't it. All support of Obote is in the north. He wishes to kill all of us in the south so these commanders, they give their orders even in the other Luo language just to Acholi, Langi, Itesos and so on.

In the midst of all this there was a letter from Austen waiting for me in Poste Restante. It was weeks old and had gone from pillar to post. It said he'd worked a 220-hour month then gone fishing.

Took off for the Embu side of Mt Kenya to the Thiba fishing camp & stayed 4 nights. Rondavels just the same & still only 5 bob a night & the hyraxes screaming and creaking at each other from 9 till 11. River's medium high. Fished the Nyamindi and Thiba Rivers from dawn to after dark with my old friend John Miano. Got the best I've ever caught – a two pound rainbow. John, of course, outdid me with a four pounder. We took the jiko & charcoal & just roasted the day's catch over the grill. Rivers are poorly stocked but fish are still catchable if you work at it. Flies that work best are Coachman, Royal Coachman, Mrs Simpson mainly, but grasshopper when desperate. Came back feeling filled with vitality. When/if you come next time bring rod & reel & we'll go together . . .

The Sikh temple near Kampala market was taking travellers again. Half a dozen of us gathered on the roof that night and listened to the shooting. A Canadian told me that Dinkas in Sudan threw spears at the truck he was on. Dave from Brixton shagged his girlfriend in a sleeping bag. An American girl asked an Asian boy why so many Asians came to East Africa.

— I've noticed a lot of Indians, she said. It's weird.

— We like the climate and have friends here, he said.

— Yeah but you know, she said, in the States we've got Chinese, Filipinos, you know, etcetera, but no Indians. Why?

— We have no friends. It's too far and we don't know about the climate.

— But I thought it had something to do with the British, she said.

— No. Our families are here.

I joined in and managed to stop the conversation dead.

— Cowboys and Indians don't get on, I said. You came here as drafted labour to build the railways. Coolies, the lunatic express.

They'd never heard of it.

Feast days at the temple were Fridays when long tables were spread with Indian food. You could eat all night while poor Ugandan women lined up outside with their nine children. The leftovers were shared out into empty milk cartons, even to old drunkards and lean prostitutes. But this was a Monday so we scraped by on bananas and groundnuts.

Next morning I tried the station and found there was a train on Wednesday going to Tororo, then north as far as it could get. All the travellers off the Sikh temple roof were going west to the Ruwenzoris. They wanted to see the dragons, three-foot worms and the pygmies. I said they were more likely to see armed chimps driving Mercedes.

Uganda Railways weren't selling train tickets till Wednesday but I got talking to Odhiambo, head of witchcraft in the loco shed. He explained the scam, the 'ticket ramp'. For five hundred shillings and three Rothman's he told me where some of the *Bwana Relwe* had lunch. The Travellers Rest.

I found the *Bwana Relwe* at their table by the pot plants. The waiter checked my bag for weapons then I told the Carriage Cleaning Supervisor I was interested in trains. He wasn't, not any more, he said. He was prouding, a 40-year-old, balding and paunching. They called him Shitman in the loco shed. He wore a white suit and solar topee. So I just said alright, I want a ticket. I know about the 'ramp', the ticket office always being shut. They looked at me like a fare dodger. Some of these men were British Rail trained. The sandwich course, queue management, dirty window preservation. The Welfare Officer had studied industrial relations in the UK. When he'd landed back at Entebbe he'd hired a taxi to drive him round Kampala to show off his new red suitcases filled with books and clothes from Oxford Street. To get rid of me, the Assistant Station Master whipped out his chit book and gave me a personal ticket.

I found a phone box that worked but it was like an open sewer. It took twenty-seven separate coins to get connected. The operator had the snitch plug in and said all calls were limited to three minutes. Austen picked up the phone at the Monitoring Unit.

— Bloke, where the fuck are you?

— Kampala.

— Good God! Where's Schick, in Luzira hah!

I said I didn't know but could he please check

the slugs for Tanzania radio, Swahili news bulletin, Saturday morning about nine.

It took him a minute, but it was there, prostitute shot and robbed one Greek businessman and one Italian. The local police were in charge of investigations. The prostitute was a 19-year-old girl in the Greek man's employ for two years. Police recovered the sum of twenty dollars from the scene.

— Well, I said, Schick had more than twenty dollars on him.

— I'll go down the Pub, bloke. I bet the fucker's there, Zippy on his lap, picking his fingernails with a bowie knife.

Well, he wasn't when I phoned Austen next day. And there was more news too, this *kaburu* called Sunderland had dropped in at Austen's in the meantime. Now that scared me a lot. Sunderland was a landlord, black-man's toothmarks on his fist, arms the colour of rusty tin roofs, beetroot face and a mouth like a smiling pike. For him there was only Sunderland's Law. He drove round Nairobi like a vigilante, usually with a woman in his boot, tied and gagged, a favourite way of dealing with anyone white who crossed his path or thwarted his desires: ten hours in his boot. He said things like: *I should be bathing in wild ass's milk and drinking champagne*. He had links with British Intelligence and the General Service Unit. He acted like the Sheriff of Nairobi. He was probably President Moi's hit man. He was certainly immune from prosecution. He raped English girls and left them for dead in game reserves and shot any Kenyans that came within ten yards of

128

his fences. *I want no kaffirs on my land*, he'd say. He could go anywhere in Kenya and say: *blacks weren't meant to have lightbulbs*. Report him to the police and you'd be beaten up, your house burnt down and your car stolen.

He'd driven round Austen's the day before with his boot roped down. He wondered if Austen had any dogs for sale, like a good Rhodesian Ridgeback with teeth like a crocodile and a taste for black men's balls, township oysters he called them. Austen coped with anyone. A good slap on the back, a guffaw, get the beer out, tell a story, sell him a dog. Sunderland mentioned Schick, matter of factly, and me, less matter of factly.

— Where's that gigolo of your wife's then?

— Fuck knows, Austen said. Had the bloody army out looking for him once and they never found him.

— Well there's more than the bloody army looking for him now Austen, Sunderland said. He went off with Schick didn't he? Well Schick's having a funeral. I've just had a talk with his brother, man called Luke Martelli, Admiral Doris they call him in the Pentagon.

The story was that Schick's 'brother' flew into Nairobi in US military transport less than twenty-four hours after the 'Italian' was shot. He gave his rank as admiral. A bunch of them had driven up to Kiambu, sealed off Schick's tea bungalow, thrown Zipporah out and shipped every board, bullet and bug, every ant, charcoal dust and lacquered doobry from floor to chimney pot, down to the plane and back to the Pentagon.

Austen said he'd go up there. If the bungalow was gone it was trouble, if not it was just Sunderland reading too many spy novels again. Ten hours in his boot and he'd forget about me. I said I was getting the train north and leaving Africa via Sudan, but I'd try and find a working phone before Easter.

— Go to Joy's, bloke. She's on your way, up at Atiak, outside Gulu. She'll have contacts . . .

On my way to the station a bomb went off in South C Street. Everyone went down like one big curtsy, like the fuckin Pope had come to town. A shop-keeper pulled me into his doorway and told me to duck behind his tea–chest counter. For ten seconds there was total silence as a slow plume of puff-ball smoke rose over the taxi park. Then a woman screamed and the crowd rose and shucked in a hun-dred directions. The shopkeeper started packing his wares into sacks.

— What's happening? I said.

— Pull the door quick, he said. And you girls, be helping me.

The girls said they just wanted to buy a *busuti* for their mother to wear to church on Easter Sunday. Someone banged on the door and shouted:

— Eh-eh Stanley, the sodjers are looting.

Stanley said we must hurry and put the sacks in the back yard.

— The sodjers they are blowing off their bombs everyday to make us Buganda panic, but everyone knows it is Obote who panics.

The day before, Obote had gone on the radio

and warned the people if they voted against the UPC they'd pay for it. He said he'd done everything the IMF and the World Bank had told him to, yet all he got was chicken feed. He said he was making that broadcast just for the record, in case he was overthrown.

The train was like the last one out before the end of the world. Passengers had their best chairs, their goats, bikes, drums of butter oil, sacks of maize and sugar. One man had three boxes of old newspapers and a six-foot lamp stand. All the doors were left open and soldiers with rocket launchers stood on the running plates and on buffers between wagons, in the goods wagon, the open freight wagon and the cab. I sat in the doorway with my feet dangling from the steps as we inched up the track at fifteen miles per hour, the klaxon clearing hundreds of people off the rails as we went. Police with clubs beat people off as they tried to grab hold of the carriages. Now and then we stopped so the stow-aways who'd jumped on the engine could be cuffed and chased into the banana groves. A lot of fares were still pocketed and no one knew how far the train would get.

The man sitting next to me said the train was secure and might go as far as Lira, his home town. He said he was Army Intelligence himself, trained in Ethiopia by the Russians, but that even he'd had his Mercedes stolen by soldiers so he'd had to take this train. These days he was working with in-flight security, Uganda Airlines. He said that so many weep-ons were carried on internal flights by soldiers and policemen that an intricate system of tagging and logging serial numbers had to be undergone before take-off, so the right guns were returned to their owners. Boarding procedure took longer than the actual flight.

— What's in it for you? I said.

Well, this bit sounded authentic at least. He didn't return with the plane. Sometimes the plane didn't come back for a month and he'd be stranded at the London Hilton on £100 sterling expenses a day. He didn't really look like a hundred-pound-a-day man. The shoes were always a giveaway. His were cracked and worn, Bata shoes which came off a dead man.

By Soroti we were all just a pair of shoes away from being dead men. The soldiers turned us off and the train was terminated. My Army Intelligence friend shuffled away to sleep the night in cardboard city like the rest of us.

Next day, there were sixty of us on the back of a tipper truck continuing north in the searing heat, shuddering along seventy-four miles of corrugated dirt to Lira, jaws smashing together on our back teeth. Then a torrential downpour under swirling black skies flooded the truck and turned the dust to mud. I'd found nothing to eat in Soroti. I was jammed against some goats so the few bananas I had in my jacket pocket were mashed to a pulp. I had some groundnuts wrapped in a twist of Bank of Barudi scrip showing the Jinja Sanitary Stores account charges for September 1971, but they rolled and scattered on the truck bed and were squabbled over by chickens with their legs tied to their wings. During the downpours the men squatted quite still like ducks and stared at their feet. The women held small shields ripped from cardboard boxes over their heads, eyes closed, sitting feet crossed. I just bowed my head like a horse and the rain ran down my neck, a far cry from a man on his way to meet his future wife.

THIRTEEN

Money was low, but there were primroses in the lanes. It was still winter, a wet last week in February. One afternoon I flogged off some of Juliette's china to an antique dealer in La Ferté Macé. Back home I filled the Land Rover with pink stove diesel, chipped the muck off my boots and doused them in hot water. After a smear of saddle soap they were decent, evening dress. I even found some brown trousers without any frayed edges. The tweed jacket was stale with mothball and clove-orange, an old London tube ticket in the breast pocket, and a bill from a Scottish shoe-menders.

At 11 p.m. I drove through slop and had to stop twice to clean the windows and rub the oil off the wipers. I put a Leadbelly tape on the cassette but the roar of engine drowned him out. I hesitated at the Athis junction, wondering if I should take the long way round, but I carried on and there they were, *les poulets*, standing by the blue van at the Briouze roundabout, my head *pandore* on night duty. He went to wave me on but flipped his hand over on impulse and pointed to the verge, his tiny hand in tiny black gloves. He'd have to get his shoes muddy, I was right-hand drive. I'd heard so many stories about *gendarmes* breathalising the sober English wife in the left-hand passenger seat while the husband sat slumped forward with his coat over the steering wheel, pickling in his wine fumes. It was the first time I'd ever been breathalised but I'd only drunk multi-vitamin fruit juice. I asked if they'd caught the burglars. No no, he said, they were far away. He didn't check the tyres or wonder why the vehicle smelled like a cooker. He must've puzzled over where I was going at that time of night in the filth, but there was only one place open if you weren't driving homewards, and it should've given him the perfect motive for the break-in: *He needed the money for gambling.*

Outside the casino at Bagnoles de l'Orne was a big sandwich board. *Grand Concert! Avec en vedette internationale LE CHANTEUR DAVE!* Free entry. Dave's cardboard cut-out was getting soggy in the drizzle. A face-lift crooner in white, a cruise-liner cabaret star, he was appearing one night only with Rita Farina and her brother Fabrice.

The bouncers ignored me, big southerners with moustaches and tight evening gear giving them indigestion. In the piano-bar some desolate couples shuffled across the floor. I thought they were pissed or just spa-town *curistes* trying to make their way to the toilets without wetting themselves till I realised it was the dance floor. A hostess in her forties with a fishnet bra was looking for shy men to buy her a drink.

Bagnoles was a whitewashed spa town surrounded by peasant farms. It was the dead of winter so half the apartments were closed down, long windows shuttered in metal like gun lockers, the few doctors who stayed on half-pay. The freezing lake was the colour of discarded bandage and lit with orange lights. It was a town which flickered between dead and alive. Even pizzeria owners went bust and became local farmers instead. Twice a year a gang of thieves with number plates from the Sarthe or Loire-Atlantique would break into a jewellery shop. It might've been a fashionable, bourgeois spa in its heyday, but the big hotels were shabby and damp and there was rubbish in the streets and farmers still came through with tractors and carts spilling dung.

It was the town where Juliette Macé spent the last five years of her life after abandoning Le Haut Bois. Drinking spring-water, she flopped in mud baths and eked out the pill-assisted minutes in the casino. Maybe it was the dream of all Juliette Macés to escape the farm and end their days there, drinking the waters with their new Parisian friends, going to the casino with retired railway officials in evening wear. Tonight, just for luck or synchronicity, I carried a keepsake of Juliette in my pocket, a note she'd pressed into the pages of her farm accounts: *Bijou's the most beaut'ful horse in the commune.*

The room I wanted was where all the punters were, pulling one-armed bandits, the *machines à sous*. A hundred shovellers, half of them like Juliette, off the valium for the night and hobbling about on canes. These were the *curistes* gambling their health insurance, fit enough to play four machines at once, wearing white trousers and slippers, too frightened to die in their beds.

The others looked mothballed, like me in a way.

136

Queuing at the lucky machines, sickly people in overcoats they last wore thirty years ago to their son's wedding. Concussed looking youths with yellow skin and long fingernails. Old farmers who lived alone.

The poster on the wall said that since 1 January the previous year 'they took their chance and won 9 462 692F'. It gave a list of the biggest jackpots and which machines had paid out and when. Anyone could see they were fixed, just from the dates. All the jackpots were on the 3, 6, 7 and 23 November and the 6, 23, 24, 25, and 30 December. The big one, 314, 817F, was Christmas Eve on the 5F machine. The second biggest, 23 December, 202, 942F, was on the 2F machine, the Wheel of Adventure, so I started there. I cashed my 200 francs for two-franc coins. One hundred adventures to go.

I'd only got 200 francs for Juliette's old stone cider jugs and a set of her china spice jars, so I felt like I was gambling her life away now. I fed the machines slowly, making time last, but not Juliette's money. I lost Juliette that night too, and for the first time I wondered where she was actually buried.

I got in at 4 a.m. stinking of smoke, sat at the table with a pot of coffee, Juliette's pink enamelled pot with the flower pattern, and wrote out the list of stolen articles and their value. I just made it up now, greedy for those thousands and thousands of francs that would get me away from Le Haut Bois. The sun came up like a rotted orange on a fruit machine, third biggest jackpot of the year.

In a sour dawn light I went outside and started digging. The depth of one shovel blade and up she came, Juliette's life in costume-jewellery, veterinary bottles, batteries, candle stubs, broken pencils, table forks, sardine tins, footscrapers, medicine, all along the fence by Aunay's field and round the cherry tree roots. Medicine from the days of liquid in glass bottles to bubble packs of psychotropic capsules. Like scattering your ashes before you're dead.

We'd known by our first winter that Le Haut Bois would be a hopeless undertaking. Whatever we pulled down just created a pile of rubble and corregated tin. We simply moved these rubbish dumps round the yard from one place to another, till in the end we covered them by inventing some feature. We ended up doing a dozen things instead of one, each task leading unnecessarily to another. By spring an intestine of nettles invaded everything we'd done.

I'd found nothing of Marcel's along Aunay's fence, so I left off digging and went to look for one of his wallets. They were scattered all over the farm. I wanted the one he'd had as a young soldier in the early thirties. I found it in the tackroom, in a rotten wooden feed trough under enamel cooking pots with the bottoms rusted out. 1st Company, 39th Infantry Regiment, Rouen, class of 1930. Hair: dark chestnut, eyes: dark blue, forehead: large vertical, nose: rectiliniar, visage: long, height: 1m 66. The two photographs had crinkly edges and showed Marcel in his early twenties, shaped like a sack even then, early spring in the public gardens. His election

138

card gave him as voter no. 62, born 16 April 1910 at Le Bisson, Menil-Gondouin, just a stroll from Le Haut Bois. He must've known Juliette already because of a postal order for fifty francs. The counterfoil was there. Address of sender: Widow Geslin, Ste-Hilaire-de-Briouze. Juliette's mother.

Marcel had a farmer's war. His papers were in cardboard hat boxes along with the black hats. He was wounded and demobbed at Carcassonne in 1940. Three days later he was back in Briouze, paying his eight hundred francs for the taxman's rubber stamp on the back of his demob papers. Then he crossed the road and visited the gendarmerie for another rubber stamp signed by Le Gendarme Desmois. By 24 May 1940, the mayor issued him a certificate of accomodation which certified that Juliette, his wife, was able to receive and accommodate him in his convalescence. So, that made it Juliette's farm. She was the inheritor when Desiré Lecoeur died. And Juliette must've brooded for thirty years over the fact that she'd die with only one living relative to inherit, Prodhomme's wife, who'd put it on the market before Juliette was even cold. That must've simplified her responsibility, spreading her widow's weeds like nettles round the yard. I'd've let the place go to rot and ruin under those circumstances too.

Aunay came later that morning, riding in the wooden cart behind the tractor, a bullock in there with him. His daughter drove and his gnarled wife rode side-saddle in the cab, rubbing her mitts together and pulling a scarf up over her head. The son-in-law belched black smoke behind in his Renault chicken shed.

Aunay walked over to the fence and pointed to one of my saplings.

— That won't grow here, he said, scraping black leaves out the wooden stream-fed trough.

They dug ditches all day with old tools, trying to drain the marshy hollows in their tiny fields. Then they hogged in fence posts with a great cartoon mallet from an oak log two feet in diameter. They used pre-war tandem saws to trim overhanging boughs. The banging went on through rain and sleet, well into darkness. Come midnight, I saw the orange tractor light still turning in the mist and bitterness.

I woke at 3 a.m. and looked across the field. A torchbeam swiped the inside of their barn window, just a fragment of glass blocked with sacking. They must've been sleeping in there because they'd turned the beasts out. The beasts were all down by my fence coughing and cotting through the stog at the water trough. I could hear the snort and flop of steaming dung. They bellowed in the soggy air like ships' fog horns. I fell asleep like Jonah in a cow's belly.

FOURTEEN

Lira was wet, dark and packed with soldiers and people in transit. I climbed off the Soroti truck as night fell and followed the men into the New World Bar & Restaurant. I found a backless chair at a filthy table, sticky from sweet tea sloshed by drunkards.

— Hey you, *mzungu!* the waiter shouted. What is it you are wanting here? *Kahawa*? Coe-fee?

Then three UNLA soldiers appeared in the doorway. Torn fatigues, one in a buttonless police raincoat, another with no tunic buttons or laces, the tongues on his boots flapping like panting dogs. They came round demanding cigarettes. The man beside me lurched sideways and poked me on the arm.

— Hey *mzungu*. Good evening sir. Yes, do you know this man, Father Grimble? Aiyee, he is, this true, a great man of Uganda pipple. Is TRUE. YES. A *mzungu* from God! He titch me to this way enjoy the sport fighting.

I knew about Father Grimble, of course. Using his name on forged testimonials got me through most Ugandan roadblocks. Everyone in Uganda knew of Grimble. He was one of Mill Hill's 'little Popes in the Bush'. His reputation had spread from South Africa to Egypt. His career was a Ugandan myth. A Sisyphus, he'd stuck it out after Independence,

141

learning the art of fighting first. He became a boxing coach and referee, training schoolboy boxers for the Commonwealth Games. His acolytes called him a dedicated innovator, giving his life to that 'wide diffusion of better principles', a Christian educator who produced sophisticated Africans equipped for a modern urban civilisation, who could take their place in a white man's world without awkwardness. Like one of his girls who got a job at the perfume counter in Harrods. He didn't want to turn out clever savages who'd strip the treasury or plot the *coup d'etat*. But everyone except the Catholic Church knew Grimble brutalised his Africans with sarcasm and ran a boot camp, jungle parody of an English public school.

The man praising Grimble raised his fists and shadow boxed, grotesquely balanced on his chair. The soldier with the flappy boots began to rise, so I did too and tried making the door.

— YOU, sit! Dog Boots shouted. I will titch him now his manners.

I was out and walking straight over the road and into the Lango Hoteli. The bar was full of prostitutes and more drunks. Some of the drunkest were fellow travellers off the Soroti truck. I paid for a room but the manager said there was no key and the room would be occupied till I wanted to sleep. He said to give him my rucksack but I said no and stood back outside. Fellow passengers huddled in groups among the hundreds of travellers stretched along the street, all waiting for the one miracle truck to take them home for Easter. They'd come from Kampala, Jinja,

Kenya, Tanzania, squatting there for days because they couldn't afford the price of a ride which doubled from one day to the next.

The Lango Hoteli had no food, just *wargi*. I walked from one cafe to the next but all they had were boiled bones and guts or just the empty boiled water. I tried the open shops, the bars, the street vendors, any smoking oil lamp on the ground beside a square of filthy rag, in case there might be three onions, a warty tomato or even a *matoke* branch. I was as hungry as Dog Boots now, nauseated from the stench of piss and rotting skins and sweating in the cold damp air, eyes stinging from charcoal smoke. I went to bed hungry but I slept well despite the men who argued half the night in the corridor over the division of women and the price of oblivion. I woke early because the barman had told me, in secrecy, that a truck was leaving for Gulu at after 1 o'clock, which meant 6 a.m.

— After one o'clock, he'd said, you ask for Mr Mbitu. You say him: Samuel is your friend.

At 6 a.m. I re-packed my damp clothes, broken shaving mirror, dented soap. A tube of shaving cream had split over two shirts and cacked up my notebook. The hotel doors were still bolted and barred from the night before. A soldier, one of Dog Boots' drunken *mshenzi*, was slumped on a Langi stool by the door, rifle between his knees. I rattled the bar. The soldier coughed and rubbed his eyes in the sunlight which slanted through a slit of window. He blew snot onto the floor with his fingers.

— It is lock-it, he said, sleepwalking over to the

143

large double doors and aiming a kick. Very lock-it, yes?

— Where is the manager? I said.

The soldier changed from sleepy drunk to guard dog with a gun. I'd talked with a soldier like him once, asked him why he was a soldier, sick, drunk, no pay, no food, no commanding officer, waking up with the pox and a hangover every morning, turned out of barracks to chase bandits who'd kill him soon enough. He'd said he was lured into the army when he'd been a gatekeeper at an Italian mission where Veronese priests had taught him to be a car mechanic. Lured into it by a uniform and a gun, rations, women and the rewards which were there for the picking if he vowed to kill his mother when ordered. He took the vow, then he was immersed in a barrel of water for several nights. This proved he was a soldier. It was the only training he got.

The mirror behind the bar was miraculously un-damaged. The soldier looked in it and ran his fingers under his ears and across his lonely yellow eyes.

— Eeh, he said, waving a backhand at the door. The manager is sick.

— How do I get out then?

This soldier was special security, sent north to infiltrate hotels and report on suspicious guests with 'much goods'. He extracted things and sold them. At the bars he guzzled as much *enguli* as he could before passing out.

He examined the door and unslid the bolts, but-ting it with his shoulder. The wooden bar along the bottom began to crack so he kicked it clear and

144

pushed hard enough to create a gap between the two doors. We saw bright sunlight on the mud outside, and an iron padlock swinging like a church bell on a heavy chain slung frame to frame.

— Oh my God, he said. He tried to wedge the gap wider with the wooden bar. We are prisoners in this sick man's hotel. Who did this?

He stepped back two paces and picked up his rifle. He put the muzzle against the padlock, stepped back another two, one more, then one forward. Final measurements, then back again. He closed his eyes and I dived for cover in the corner, clamping my hands over my ears. There were two rapid bursts. The door was splintered good and the mud outside was cratered. There were feet flying down the road and voices everywhere. The smell was sharp and bitter but the padlock still held. He'd fuckin missed. He butted the padlock twice with the rifle and the chain slid free. He kicked the door out, floundering into the mud and the firing line of four soldiers running towards him with rocket launchers at the ready.

— S'okay s'okay, he shouted and waved his hand like at flies.

When I poked my face outside he was pissing like a horse against the wall.

— Come, he said. Get out. It is open.

— Thank you, I said, walking out and trying to get as far away as I could before he let go of his cock and picked up that rifle again.

— Hey *mzungu*, he said still pissing. You give me one stick.

I should've done that without being asked so I threw him a crushed packet of Sportsman with three sticks left. As he moved to catch it his rifle slid sideways and he pissed on it.

I waited for Mr Mbitu's truck in Speke Street, propping myself on a raised boardwalk. A tailor came out to see what the shooting was. I told him.

— Ah, these ones, he said.

He fetched a treadle Singer outside. The women were still wrapped in their bedrolls. Downhill at the Caltex station I could see fifty vehicles which had queued all night for petrol rumoured to be on its way from Mombasa. At the front of the queue was a Uganda Caltex petrol tanker with a soldier at the wheel. I asked the tailor if Mr Mbitu's lorry was in the queue.

— Yes, he said. This one.

— Where?

— The green Tata lorry which he stole from Mr Patel who owned the petrol station.

The green Tata lorry was at the back, last in the queue, next to a dead dog with its head crushed inside a cloud of flies. Mr Mbitu was sitting with his bare feet dangling out the cab.

— *Jambo*, I said. Mr Mbitu, Samuel is my friend.

— Welcome. Where are you coming from?

— Will you get petrol today? I said.

Mr Mbitu wore a white Muslim's cap and *kalimu*.

— *Inshallah*, he said. You see this petrol lorry in the front? The soldiers will fill for themselves.

— Fill what? Their tank?

— Yes.

— The whole lorry or the petrol tank?

— Yes, all of it. There will be remaining for us nothing. We can buy the petrol from the soldier.

— Are you going to Gulu?

— Yes. One thousand shilling or two thousand shilling.

On a corner of Speke Street there was a branch of the Uganda Commercial Bank. I needed the official stamp and some currency on my Exchange Control Form or there might be trouble at the border with Sudan. It was mid-morning. Inside the bank I took a ten-dollar bill from my money belt and handed it to the clerk. He read it front to back then rolled it into a thin stick and walked idly across the floor. All the other tellers and customers stopped what they were doing and watched. The assistant manageress sat with two clients at her windowside desk, a portrait of the President behind her.

— Uh? was all she said to the clerk.

— Ten US, he said.

She didn't disguise her contempt at the paltry bill. She opened a drawer and wet-thumbed a small pile of low denomination Uganda Bank notes. She handed the ten-dollar bill to her assistant at the next desk and he held it up to the light, flexed the corners, snapped it tight a few times. She waited. He nodded his approval and the clerk wandered back over and presented me with the wad of chaffed notes.

— Count them here, he said. They are three thousand shillings, yes?

— So many? I said, and slid the Exchange Control Form across the counter.

The clerk stubbed his finger on it.

— Why are you bringing this here?

— I must have it stamped.

— My friend, this business is unofficial.

He slid the form back.

— You want only one hundred seven shilling? The rate today is up and down. Now it is three hundred shillings . . .

The assistant manageress was folding my ten-dollar bill square till it was the size of a passport photo. Then it disappeared through a gap in her blouse and down her bra.

— Put the notes in your pocket, the clerk said.

At midday a tipper truck stopped unexpectedly in Market Square. In ten seconds it was invisible under a swarm of bodies. One man lobbed two goats onto the roof rack above the cab. The driver revved and yelled and rocked the tipper, trying to chuck everyone off. The conductor rammed his way through the mob grabbing wads of notes off anyone with room enough to stand and pay him. In five minutes the notes were like a hod of bricks. I couldn't get anywhere near the truck so I waited, knowing what would come.

— Hey *mzungu*, the conductor said when he saw me. Where?

— Gulu, I said.

— Yes, he said, we are off to Gulu, two hundred shilling.

Gulu, a handful of dusty miles from Atiak, from Joy the gold-panning missionary. This time she'd be sweeping the beaten floor or writing in her diary or watering her sweet potatoes with last night's rain.

FIFTEEN

The insurance broker missed nothing. He wrote saying he wanted the hay clearing out the barn because it was a fire risk. If I didn't clear it in seven days, it would nullify my insurance and make my claim void.

The last cut had been twenty years back, but the end barn was still half-full of old dusty square bales. The top layer had tumbled and melded like a thatch. It had to be pitch-forked to the doorway, bundled out and into a barrow, then wheeled to the middle of the yard and piled all over again in reverse procedure.

I'd started it that Saturday afternoon when Joy said she was leaving. Then, I'd worked in a blind daze, but now I was glad to do it. It was something I *could* do, something I was good at and it would become an obsession in the weeks that followed when I cleared every barn and loft. I mulched the whole garden with it twice over, a foot thick, like laying turf. I loved the smell, the folded concertinas of past meadows, the clovers, teazles and buttercups. Now and then I'd find an object, or shrunken creature, caught by the cutter and included in the final bale. But the finds I loved most were the fresh naps of green grass perfectly preserved with a bright yellow buttercup or fairy flax or wild poppy. It was like the breeze had turned that old barn dust to pollen, and

I was standing in a field of hot green summer grass, watching the apples grow back in the last year Le Haut Bois was a working farm.

After two days pitching the barn began to empty and in several places I hit the floor. Here the hay was compacted and red with the texture of under-bark, white mushroom spores and dry rot. The rat warrens were like raised veins where the thin lime screed crumbled into the beaten clay and the rain had followed the rats in.

In the top left corner of the barn beside the lane, level with the main beam on the 'A' frame, there were several bales still grouped to form a hidden seat within a dip. It was there I began to cry one winter afternoon, face muffled in the hay, and this became an event I actually began to look forward to. I'd go in there, pull the door shut, climb up to my place quite calmly, then sit and wait, like I was expecting a lover. Crying released chemicals and hormones, stretched glands and pulled at muscles. It was emo-tional training, but whoever said 'have a good cry' forgot about the ones you have to have before they get anywhere near good, like those which begin in abysmal confusion. There's nothing worse than thinking you're on top of a particular moment, then finding you're not, especially if you're out in the garden, or driving away from the house on an errand which is supposed to take your mind off things. Crying then was like being sick, a poison or pus which built up hot behind the eyes, forcing me to pull over quick or rush into the hay barn. My armpits stretched and twisted and I got hot clean eyes and itching all over my body, and this thumping tinitus like a stretched drum skin shuddering in the left ear. But gradually, I began to accomplish it with a shrug, just moving aside, sticking my hands in my pockets and standing there sobbing till it was over and I could go back out again, like one of those wooden boys on a weather clock.

Then one day, when the last plank burned on the fire and the yellow wind slammed a corrugated iron sheet against the wall and the rain barrel split in two from ice six feet thick, I went outside to muck out the goats and fetch wood. I ended up weeping against the barn door, great shuddering sobs, as the geese strutted round the yard like German troops searching the barns for stowaways. I stood drying my eyes with the backs of dirty rough hands, looking at the galoshes floating in the scummy water trapped under the cider press. One galosh frozen, half sunk into a lump of jagged ice, the other floating like a drowned dog. The air was like a sheet of filthy glass. Chaffinches fell out the mist and landed briefly, pecked at soggy or frozen bread, then disappeared in a flit of the wing. And that's when I saw Aunay standing in the yard watching me.

I'd always thought of him as the sour old bastard who was sent to make my life as miserable as his own. At first, when he'd walked all over our property and criticised everything we did, I'd stand there dumb and smiling, leaning on some resurrected implement so he'd think I had some rural authenticity of my own, some right to be there. I pretended I understood and even made sure to have mud on my face. Then as this image slipped away before him, we clung faithfully to the notion that we were privileged to witness an authentic peasant mark out the last days of agrarian poverty at our fence. Only the harder we'd worked, the more he'd interfered, and soon, if I heard the tractor coming I'd retreat into the barn and watch through cracks in the cob till he'd gone up into their fields and it was safe to come out.

Then after Joy quit, I listened out for his tractor differently, looking forward to it, thinking maybe there was something we could learn from each other before it was too late. But now the time had come to consider it, I felt like I was weeping for him too. I'd seen men in suits measuring his fields, putting their wellingtons into plastic bags before they got back into their smooth grey cars. We'd witnessed each other's failures, misunderstanding it for something else, but we both knew the other had reached the end.

It was late February in the yellow-grey six o'clock light when the insurance man called again and caught me weeping. I'd put the animals away so there was no warning, just a knock at the door. I stepped through the hole in the wall to the kitchen and cut an onion in half, rubbed it over my hands and went to the door holding knife and onion, wiping swollen eyes. How long he might've stood at the door who knows, or even if he was fooled. He was pestering for more proof that the stolen items existed. I didn't have receipts so he wondered if I had photographs with any of the items visible. I said no. I'd already looked, but somehow nothing ever got in the photos. But he wasn't satisfied, insisting I get some out and check again.

Of all the pictures to turn up first, there was Joy sitting on the stolen bench by the woodstove in the orange sunlight of a September afternoon. She's only a small portion of the picture but I can see her mug of tea, the buttons on her white cord breeches, her silk shirt under a Peruvian jumper. She's looking happy too, but I'm trying to skip round her with my eyes looking for more stolen objects. There were other photographs of that day, even one of the stolen table but with a cloth on it. Our rucksacks are visible too, packed to bulging and propped on the chairs. We were waiting for a lift to the ferry, going to London for the winter. It had been the countdown to the end of us. After a month I insisted we come back to Le Haut Bois. She came with me, stayed three weeks then left.

And now this insurance git in his maroon suit and yellow tie, his perfumed collar and padded leather briefcase, wanted to see the tablecloth so he could measure it. I laid it on the floor and pointed out the folds where the edge of the table had marked it. He drew an insurance man's picture of it in his notebook.

A friend's wife Cecile came round the same week. The study curtain was open, tied to a ribbon pinned to the window frame, so I could watch the evening darken as I made tea and fried a cheese sandwich in a skillet. I don't know what I saw that evening, maybe the tiled roof on the cob *porcherie*, remembering how we re-tiled it together in our first spring. I stood by the window and started untying the ribbon to let the curtain fall across, but I couldn't undo the knot for tears. As I wiped them away, there was Cecile standing outside and looking up, at what was probably my shadow, I don't know. She still knocked, perhaps to let me think she hadn't seen me. I'd cut onion rings for the skillet, so I cut some more and shouted *come in*. Cecile tried the key hanging in the lock till I opened it myself, knife and onion in hand. I even said: *I'm peeling onions, look*, leaving the tears on my face to prove it. She'd been to the park with her three kids. She was just passing, wanted to see if I was, you know, okay and that. She knew. I could see that now, but I still denied it in front of her, while remembering what she'd said the week Joy left. I said Joy had had to go to Africa. Cecile said *Really, she's gone? I never thought she would.*

There's always someone who knows. This afternoon, Cecile had come to admit she'd had an aerogramme with giraffes on the stamp which I made her fetch from the car and recite to me. Apparently Joy had never been happy until she'd left me. Game over. I never cried another drop.

PART 3

SIXTEEN

St Luke's Guest House in Gulu was on the road to Juba, Pakwach and West Nile. Daniel kept it as a Living Christian Meeting House, holding Bible study behind a bamboo partition. He was a short bald man who'd worn the same blue suit every day for twenty years. Once a year he sent it to a tailor who stitched and contrived another twelve months out of it. People said it was the only miracle Daniel would ever see. He wore the spectacles he'd been given by the mission, but he'd never changed the lenses. He said his eyes had grown into them now, the way you grow into the Lord if you receive him and you're compatible with his spirit. He trusted everyone.

Some days, the international post brought him evangelical pamphlets from America. They were mostly in Swahili so he cycled round the district handing them out, a St Luke's nameplate hanging from his crossbar. The latest batch were from the World Missionary Press, Indiana. *Published as the Lord provides the means in more than 130 languages . . .* Yellow booklets the size of handbag mirrors, with literal translations like: *The Lord comes like virginal snot from the clouds . . .* Booklets about three characters called Mungu, Kristo and Benji who could've been three Disney dogs spreading the word of *Bwana*.

As Daniel booked me in he handed me one.

— No thanks Daniel, I said.

Daniel wore new plimsolls with his blue suit and he was smiling like a Halloween pumpkin. I picked on St Luke's because it was clean and Daniel was obviously scrupulous in his duties. I unpacked half my stuff and Daniel said it was alright to leave it because he owned strong keys and this was a Christian place.

— That won't save us, I said.

— You are anyways welcome.

There was a notice pinned to the wall inside the gate so I went out and read it. It was a Pest Control Endorsement Card. Even with Uganda in ruins, Gulu sent round its mosquito inspector. He'd called the previous week and stamped his all-clear mark. He'd also done so for the entire period of Amin's dictatorship.

Opposite St Luke's, a crowd in transit waited under a mango tree and an uncertain sky. I went back inside and looked for Daniel.

— How far is Atiak? I said.

— You wait with us in the mission house, he said. Let me find some means for you when there is someone going that way.

I was too restless for St Luke's so I sat in the New Suitable Cafe because it was opposite the lorry park. It was selling orange juice done in the blender, and fresh cake. The cake was dry and heavy, yellow wonders-will-never-cease cake made from stolen flour and baby-milk powder. After an hour I stood by the lorry park, an empty half-acre of dust and cinders. I could see the horizon half a mile away, a slight rise to the south-east. A UN lorry swished past ignoring me. Then a Land Rover with two white women parked a small way down the street so I strolled down and asked for a lift.

— We're only going to Pakwach.

— No good for Atiak then, Pakwach?

— Atiak? one of them said. You must be barmy going that way right now.

— Why's that?

— West Nile's swarming with soldiers. There won't be much going through. Sorry.

I went back to the lorry park. The sun burned through the cloud. The hours dragged by. There was a petrol station next to me. Burnt-out pumps and blackened stanchions, windows boarded with old doors from derelict shops. I walked down into the shade of the few shops nearby. Their shelves were tea chests stacked open end out. The dark wooden counters still had brass measures screwed down. One shop had three packets of *Simba Chai*, the other some jars of petroleum jelly and plastic zips. From round the back the thin scrape of a tranny tuned to hi-life from Zaire. I sat on the boardwalk the rest of the afternoon, jack-eyed at the shimmering road, kicking myself when I realised I should've asked the white women if one of them was Joy.

The radio finally died. The Flying Eagle batteries took a dive late afternoon when people began to reappear as the air cooled. I heard the low grinding of gears, the long deceleration of a big lorry coming over the brow in a shimmer of haze caught by the full slant of setting sun. What would I do if this lorry was going north into Sudan? If I jumped on it, there'd be no point in getting off at Atiak. Juba was only a day away. In Juba I'd be safe. I didn't want to risk stumbling into a nest of soldiers at Atiak, Joy or no Joy. And if she wasn't there I'd be foolish, and probably dead.

There was no more time to weigh the question. The long bright-orange bonnet reared into Gulu, grinning chrome. As it slowed, two soldiers jumped off the running board. I ran alongside shouting:

— Juba? Juba?

— No man, the mate shouted back. Pakwach.

— Ah fuckin hell, what's at Pakwach, gin? Beer?

— There is nothing. You do not want to go there. You wait, a lorry he is coming. Eeee Pakwach, little village, no even a town. Nowhere to sleep, just with sodjers . . .

Church bells rang at twilight. An old man on sticks shuffled home as a stiff breeze ruffled the mango tree by the verge and blew dust in my eyes. With the sudden darkness of low cloud it began to rain. I set off for the verandah outside the Tourist Inn and Lodge at the back of the empty bus park. The rain stopped before I got there.

— There are no buses now, the lodgekeeper said.

— Were there ever any buses?

— Oh yes, many beautiful buses, English buses. We have many rooms.

— No, I have a room.

I couldn't face an early night at St Luke's, so I

162

sat smoking and listening back at the lorry park. A passer-by said I should move into the light for safety. I mustn't sit in the dark. The only light came from a pink neon sign hanging from string on the cake-maker's wall. The electricity had come on at sunset and would go off at midnight. Another voice asked me for matches.

— Give me sigara . . . one stick . . . give me shillings . . . I want dollar . . .

Every time I asked, the answer was the same. There is no transport. You won't get means. Perhaps tomorrow it is coming. You must go to the hotel now.

Easter Sunday, the morning grey as cardboard. At nine the entire guest roll of St Luke's was led to church by Daniel. Even some of those waiting for transport went along to church. I stood outside and saw two lorries pass. Lira, the word went round. Two *wazungu* in yellow windcheaters stood in the back of one among the few imports, sacks and pots and waste paper. The driver refused to stop.

The Biblebacks reappeared and I stood at the gate till Daniel had changed into plimsolls.

— What's happening with the means, Daniel?

— The means, they will return. You wait and we can get them.

A soldier walked up to me as Daniel went inside.

— Stick.

I gave him a Sportsman and he snatched it up to his mouth. He said he was from the border post near Arua.

— You come with me. I have a jeep.

The Sportsman jerked up and down as he spoke.

— No, thank you.

He spat on the road and stared at it, like he was looking for blood. There was a lot of TB in Northern Uganda. I avoided looking at his gob, or the soldier. He began striking one useless match after another. I wasn't getting my windproof lighter out for this bastard to pinch, only I had to show a modicum of respect as he might be important if he really had a jeep. His tunic was buttoned high, plain, scrubbed out green, army surplus, no markings, just a red badge on his cap which might've been the fuckin Scouts for all I knew.

— I am an officer, the soldier said. You are journalist, isn't it.

— No, of course not, I said. Why do you say that? Here, keep the packet, I said, handing him the bloody fags and unzipping my escape pocket at the same time. I brought out an old Kenyan Tax Card I'd got in Nairobi Market, a blank on to which I'd typed my name and occupation.

— Look, you see. I am a teacher in Kenya.

The soldier seemed impatient for something. Perhaps not for me, but I knew he'd gladly catch me up in it.

— Ah, he spat again. This time I looked at it. Bloodless. It is your business, he said. It is the same.

I walked towards the lorry park. Halfway up the high street I heard the rittling of a bike bell over the pits and ruts in the road and saw a white nun on a

164

green dismantlable bike. She said good morning. The cathedral bells rang into silence, not a single machine or animal, only the pinging of the nun's Chinese bell as she disappeared round the corner. It was Easter weather too, heavy warmth rising from the crumbling earth, the sun showing through and the grey red of the empty lorry park turning dry mustard yellow. Safari ants marched in rings round pools of engine oil. The bus park was empty too, a mass of bomb craters where two vultures fought over a piece of rag.

I went for a stretch, passing by Custom Corner Mills, looking for the railway station. I turned off the Omoro Road and walked up the tracks. Some children snapped firewood from acacia trees. Where are you going? they said. I made a noise like a steam train. There were weeds between the tracks and lizards on the rails and the flies were like a black cloud hanging over me, swarming at my wet back.

A spindly boy in school shorts came running after me, his elbows hanging out of a red woollen sweater.

— Sir, he said. The train did not come this time. Many pipple wait and wait. It did not even find Lira.

I gave him a cigarette but he wanted two. He said his whole family were walking along the railway line with their belongings.

— What is a *mzungu* doing on his footies?

— Where are your belongings? I said.

— My sister is like a camel, the boy said.

In Speke Street I watched a group of pregnant women in their Easter bonnets filing to church. They wore white wraps and held garlands of brilliant

flowers in each fist. A contraption came zig-zagging
round the corner after them, a crippled boy in a
wheelchair pushed by a girl shorter than the handles.
The front bogie was snapped clean away, the other
spinning uselessly as it hit the ground. The girl
struggled to keep the chair tipped back on its big
wheels and the boy's spidery legs angled out over
the wheel arches. He glared at me in his starched
white shirt and impeccably ironed white tie pinned
to his chest.

— Good morning sir.

They stopped, the girl holding on to the wheelchair like a porter's trolley. She bowed all the way
down, almost kissing my boots.

— Goodbye sir, she said. God bless you sir.

More girls were sauntering up the middle of the
street carrying flowers, proud in their Sunday frocks,
scrubbed skin, oiled hair, ribbanded baskets adorned
in the Uganda colours. They curtsied too and said
good morning sir and God bless you sir. One of
them said:

— Are you in need of assistance sir?

— Yes, I said. Help me get out of Uganda.

I heard a truck then, turning into the bus park.
I hurried down to the corner. I thought I'd see the
truck heading off to Layibi or Bobi but it came
straight at me in a cloud of dust. A ten-ton Bedford
with three soldiers on a joyride, careening on to the
Koc road. I looked up into a pair of fuckin great
nostrils under a red cap, one hand miming a pistol
pointing right at my head, the mouth firing two
shots. They sped past Customs Corner, scattering the

166

girls, bouncing over ruts, the lorry sounding like a load of slammed doors. Then nothing for six hours, just the light breeze flicking the roadside grass and stirring the dust. The claustrophobia in Gulu was beginning to feel like an escape act gone wrong, the air running out, the water rushing in.

That night I lay on the bed asking myself: *what am I coming out of this with?* I closed my mind like it was a box of raffle tickets in the Easter Prize Draw. I sifted through, pulled one out, the brightest image of my time in Africa. I couldn't tell if I'd lost or won, because it was Nema, the Chagga girl. Was she really the central moment of my whole journey, the nearest I'd come to real contact with an African? And I didn't even know what had happened, what was real or a hoax.

When I tried to think of Joy it was Nema who stuck in my mind. If she was behind bars she'd be half kicked to death by now, or fucked into a coma. I'd soon forget her back in London, boasting like a bush stiff about all the scrapes and the tyrants and the action I'd seen. I could always go back for her. A man like Austen would. Then what would I do with Nema anyway, for chrissake? Smuggle her to Kenya and inherit Austen's pick'n'mix compound? Build her a hut from old Tanzanian coffee tins and cardboard and buy her a few chickens? She wouldn't get through UK immigration anyway, and Zanna would be right to scoff and say: *I knew one'd hang you out to dry, a little dollybird with beads.* Even if I did go back for her I wouldn't get halfway before they stuck a conspiracy charge on me. Then one night I'd disappear into Sunderland's car boot. No, it was Nema's life. Prostitution, slavery, jail. She wouldn't want me in any case, or maybe for a night or two, a few discos in Dar. She wouldn't sit at home polishing the spears and mashing *posho* while I went off on a bus to try and earn the bus fare off the World Service for, I don't know, a story about T9 dogs attacking the Manyatta District of Embu.

And Joy? Joy was an empty house. The road went to Juba, Khartoum, Cairo, Athens, Rome and London. Not Atiak. I fell asleep turning it all into song, Gene Pitney or that old blues number, I couldn't remember, about springing ma baby outa jail, or was it Yonder Miss Rosie, *Let the midnight special, shine her light on me . . .*

I woke next morning at 4 a.m. and dressed quickly, smoking as I tied my boots. My stomach chimed twelve, feeling emptier than it had all week. Redundant digestive juice shot pains like poison up into my ribs. The town cocks crowed and a bird screeched like a cat in a milk bottle. One was on the roof, and another answered from the mango tree. I peered through the window but it was too dark to see. I could hear a fist hammering on a street door and someone shuffling in the yard below my window. A standpipe dripped outside into a bucket because someone stole the washer. A spider scurried under the door, a firefly found its way in through the rush curtain.

Outside, the full moon was setting over Gulu,

168

casting a long shadow under the mango tree. The dawn breeze caught my cigarette smoke and crickets scratched in the short, dry grass. New webs were dust-covered in a dewless dawn, dry, like string, sagging with mosquitoes. The milestone read JUBA 182 miles. Even if I had to walk it.

SEVENTEEN

It was Easter when I told the broker I wanted to cancel the insurance on Le Haut Bois and get a six-month rebate on the premium. He said I couldn't do that. I was paid up till September and I had to give a year's notice.

At least the spring rain had stopped and the wind blew, drying the land and the stones in the yard, turning the silt to dust and pushing it down the lane. The fields were crammed yellow with wild daffodils, then lagoons of bluebells. The winter's toil had been cleaned up naturally and I emerged into some kind of sunlight like the bombardment was over.

I peeled back the black plastic and peered under the hay mulch on the vegetable beds and found the soil dark, loose and weedless, shaped like a lino-cut board, whole skins shed by grass snakes who'd spent their winter there. The broad beans and garlic I'd sown in November had weathered the freeze. The swallows arrived at teatime on 14 April and flew straight to their old nests in the cowshed. Marcel Macé had painted these nests with white limewash forty years ago and the swallows patched them up, rebuilding the tops every year with fresh brown mud like Arabian basketwork. The hens began laying and the goslings and ducklings took their first splash in the *mare*. I gardened by day and then, come evening, I walked along the Orne looking for wild hop shoots. Flies hatched as the water lost colour, that bitter, clay brown it scooped from eroded banks began to clear over the shallows, making the chub visible again as blue smudges between boulders.

Le Haut Bois was now worth less than Joy had paid for it. This was another poised guillotine; my name was not on the deeds. She'd bought it with money left by her mother and now I'd received written instructions from Joy's solicitor to sell it on her behalf. Simplification to the bone. The rising pound, a collapsed building, the state of the roofs. I'd already sold the clay tiles off the roofs for food, and patched them with half rusted sheets of corrugated tin which had horse shit on the undersides.

Then, the second week in May, I had more gendarmes business. I was hitching a trailer to the Land Rover and loading up all the old farm iron for this English bloke who ran a gîte in Brittany and wanted it for his garden. The hay rake and swap hook, anvils, irons, raves and so on. He said he'd give me fifty quid plus the diesel. I'd just secured the iron wheels of the rake when the gendarmes' blue *panier à salad* came down the lane in slow motion. They took their cardboard hats off and placed them on the seat, turned the volume on the old Bakelite telephone up, checked the clipboard, flicked a bee out which bounced off the inside of the windscreen. They wouldn't look at me yet, waiting till they came within that regulation three-metre circle in which they look up and say '*bonjour*'. The head *pandore* wore new shoes today, and new rings under his eyes. I knew what they wanted. They'd had a complaint that I was impersonating a police officer, all because of a catalogue I'd retrieved out the recycling bins in Briouze.

It was something I'd started doing that spring, putting my arm through the rubber flap of the recycling bin, my hand like a lucky dip grabber at the fairground. If I saw the fat glossy catalogues I'd nearly dislocate my shoulder to ease the things out. I could drool hours away on the front steps with a catalogue, a tin mug of red *picrate* from a plastic barrel at my side. A thousand-page catalogue of clean shiny lives. I dreamed of a varnished wooden hut with just the one of everything. A green and yellow plate, clear perspex pepper-mill, orange-handled knife and fork, green toaster, red curtains, duvet cover with a blue border and a big picture of sunflowers round a hut in the Var with the blue sea between mountains. I wanted sunlight, colour and the smell of lavender, Normandie FM instead of Radio 4, falafals and yoghurt instead of fried spuds and cabbage. I needed a lover, a garden, a wood to collect mushrooms and a little river full of roach and trout to start all over again. I'd keep Juliette's basket, her flower pots and a photo. She had become the woman in my life. I was her guest and lodger, in a way her only heir. In the war I'd've crossed the fields at night and she'd've stashed me in the barns under the hay when the Germans came asking questions. All spring she was more real than Joy had ever been. It was like I'd never met Joy at all, I was just waiting for Juliette to come home.

172

I still had the catalogue. French catalogues weren't free, you had to pay up to ten quid for them, so the recycling bin was the only place I could get one. I'd not seen this one before and the prices were cheaper and the quality of the goods unusually high. They offered supplements too, outdoor gear, motoring, woodstoves. There were forms inside which the previous owner had started filling in till he changed his mind. I'd filled in the request for the supplements, given my name and address and used the envelope provided. A letter came a week later saying they had no record of my existence as a French citizen or as an employee in the state sector, that the catalogue was registered to an officer of the French Gendarmerie. I looked at the order forms and yes, there was his name. Gendarme Crozier, Gendarmerie, Briouze. It was a catalogue for members of the state apparatus only.

He shook hands with me, this man who'd changed his mind about ordering an inflatable mattress with built-in foot-pump, a wooden shoe rack, foot jacuzzi and some stuff for fixing leaks on a caravan roof. Perhaps *his* wife had come back to him before he sent the order in. His shirt was ironed, he was smooth-shaven. I was still looking like Joy had just left me. He must've seen that now, five months on and she still wasn't there. He looked me in the face and put his fingers together.

— How's it going? he said.

— It goes, I said. Good weather, plenty to do.

— Good, he said. We want to know something. Did you ever see an Arab in the lane?

Still on his witch-hunt for a fuckin Arab. The Arabs lived in Flers in the HLMs. They mostly stayed there too, but any theft in the bocage was blamed on them. Farmers said they rustled sheep then slit their throats in their bathtubs. Le Pen got his name sprayed in red on bridges round Flers. The only names printed in the *Faits Divers* columns of *L'Orne Combattante*, were like El Mansouri and Mahmood Zouina, just for breaking windows in a phone box or cheating on a car sale. But a French uncle convicted of abusing his 10-year-old niece was 'a 31-year-old man'.

— No, I said. Never seen an Arab here.

— Anywhere, he said.

— Sudan, I said.

— What?

— Why, I said. Have you found something?

He shook his head repeating no about six times. Then they just stood there looking at the trailer, shifting a foot at a time towards the tyres, then abandoning caution and checking the tow hitch, the connection and the runaway brake. They asked me to test the electrics, lights, indicators. Everything worked, but they spotted an illegal tyre. Yes, I said, I was going to buy two new ones.

— Papers, please.

No road tax, insurance on an address in England I'd forgotton, Sudanese driver's licence that cost me a few *hamsa grish* and a bottle of Johnnie Walker for the examiner.

— You can't drive this vehicle, Crozier said.

The young bald *pandore* was standing by the barn

174

door now. He tried the handle and pushed but it was locked. He came back, bored by the countryside, flapping at bees and shrugging. They might've gone then if Gendarme Crozier hadn't seen his driver doing that.

— What's in the barn? he said, alert now.

I fetched the key, they poked gloveless into rusted heaps of metal, powdering wood, rags and dust, inching towards the garden tools, the cider pump, the hessian sacks, the fifty-litre Calvados barrels, and on into thickets of unidentifiable objects piled from floor to ceiling. I thought they'd seen everything in their line of work, but they looked at me with body language I had no dictionary for.

— It was her, I said. She left it like this.

— Who? Your wife?

— No, the widow, Juliette Macé.

EIGHTEEN

Dawn was a faint glow before sunrise. The people of Gulu were still coughing in their beds. I found the gaffer of the New Suitable up, boiling eggs and coffee.

— Yes, Ebrahim said, there will be means to Juba today.

This was the day I was getting out then, so I rushed breakfast. I was on the last few sips of coffee when someone hawked up outside then flagged through the doorway like he'd been walking all night. A *mzungu* in a donkey jacket. We nodded to each other and he dumped his sack at the counter and stood there pulling dead strands of beard off his chin. The spare chairs were hooked to the walls.

— *Jambo*, he said. Any *chai*?

— *Jambo*. What is it you want? Ebrahim said.

— Tea. *Chai*, man.

— There is no-thing.

— Coffee? *Kahawa? Ndio?*

— Tomorrow there is coming a little coffee, Ebrahim said.

The *mzungu* looked at me because I was drinking something hot from a plastic mug.

— Ask 'im for hot water, I said.

— Hey, cheers man. Hot water?

— Yes, Ebrahim said.

— Dry tea? Dry coffee?

— Tea leaf, Ebrahim said. Dry coffee.

— Excellent *bwana*, excellent. Hot water, dry coffee, *mkubwa*, grand, big one. What about snap?

Ebrahim walked through a doorway into the yard out back.

— Bl'dy 'ellfire, the *mzungu* said, though fuck knows why. Ebrahim came back.

— Yes, there is hot water available for refreshment.

A language war was brewing here.

— Aye, the *mzungu* said. Grand. An' snap? *Chakula?*

— Sit down, Ebrahim said. He stood on a stool and unhooked a chair from the wall and carried it over to my table.

— Here is sitting your friend. I am coming.

He left us together and we could smell charcoal smoking in the yard. The *mzungu* moved his chair out from the table and rested his elbows on the next one over, rolling three smokes in *Guardian Weekly* strips. He looked round the walls at the gloss-paint murals, long, bent tigers and hippos with elephantiasis. The menu was nailed to an old door and propped against the wall. He read it out loud.

— *Chai* ten shillings, chapatti twenty shillings, egg thirty shillings. Aye, the menu to break hearts that, but no plates eh, youth? Stomach's cut me throat an' here we are dining wi' St Anthony. Been in Gulu long, like? Smoke?

I took one of his *Guardian Weeklies*. It had the

crossword on it. 'French oboe up in trees (2,4,4).'

— Ta, I said. Three days.

— Right sewer eh? Musta killed the fish, ha. Which way yer heading?

— Khartoum, I said.

— Uh-huh.

There was no point drubbing the old subjects so we blew out newsprint and kept up the old north-south divide. I guessed he was from Nottinghamshire, the sort of bloke who'd written *DH Lawrence* on his schoolbooks instead of *Mansfield Town*. The scruffy beard, the bag made of camel gut with half the guts still hanging off it. The donkey jacket, the field boots, the hint of Marxism. Then Ebrahim came in with coffee, egg and chapatti.

— Aye oop, feast! Cor, that fer me *bwana*? Much obliged sirrah, much obliged. Half snags mate?

— I've eaten, I said.

— You are welcome, Ebrahim said, but he sounded anxious. I am telling your friend this. Go to the poli-cee station where is the lorry, yes? For Juba, this lorry is checkid first in the poli-cee check.

I asked the bloke if he wanted a lorry for Juba.

— Aye, he said. His mastications and sippings made dull blunt echoes in the dusty cafe, like a field of snicking sheep. 'Ow's thah name youth? Mine's Wesley.

— Norman, I said.

— Aye Norm, w'nt mind a lorry to Juba. I'll come up there wi'thee if yer gizza tick.

— No, I said. Take yer time. I have to go that way. There aren't no lorries in Gulu anyway.

178

I didn't want Wesley up there with me.

— Right youth. You find out the crack. See yer back here or up the lorry park? Where's yer stuff, like?

— Safe, I said. To hand.

The police station was a quarter mile away on the brow of a hill near the post office and the barracks. The hospital opposite had been commandeered by the army. There was no lorry in the police compound, just the naked flagpole, its rope cut and stolen up as far as the thief could shin. In the doorway three policemen were beating a man with a bicycle inner tube, so I sat down by the roadside to wait for the lorry and emptied the grit from my boots. They took no notice, so I pulled out my notebook. Inside was a pre-stamped postcard of a stuffed lion in the elephant grass, a dead tangled impala at its feet. *Simba, King of Beasts*, it said. I was the Augustan for a few moments, writing of the wagtails chasing butterflies, the dry cracking of the grass, sweat bees driven mad from lack of rain, the stump of rope on the flagpole and the police beating an Acholi thief in the doorway, in the shade of leafless trees. I smoked a cigarette and listened to his howls and the beaters cursing in vernacular. The lane curved away to Pongdwongo but it could've been to Benenden or Mayfield. When the rains came the verges would be lush green, but today the sky was like old dry rag dropping dust as the sun burned the edges.

There was a breeze, darkening clouds, the close air, insects abandoning their nests. The sweat bees

179

were hovering over my arms and face. I was tired. I swiped at one and it fell. They didn't sting, only you couldn't get rid of them and they stank if you crushed them on your skin. More wagtails came and feasted on the butterflies over the police station. Some soldiers disembarked nearby and a mob began to assemble in the lane. More soldiers drove by in UN lorries. Then, like a termites' nest, there were soldiers turning in and out of barracks and the air filled with shouts and revvings and the drone of vehicles. I forgot all about rain, police and transport and ran back into the township.

I saw an old cream-coloured Leyland bus with a big red stripe down its side. It trundled by then turned right, backed up, and came by again. It was empty. The turnboy walked down the aisle smoking a cigarette. Down at the *keepi-lefti* roundabout, two hundred people were gesticulating at the disappearing bus. A few men ambled up the street and shrugged at the dustcloud. A loaded truck pulled up outside the New Suitable in a series of jolts. I watched Wesley jog towards it but it sherried off again, down to the roundabout and up towards the police station. Wesley sat down in the lorry park with his back against a tree. After a few seconds he started scratching his back and legs. A safari ant came away in his fingers, head and pincers stuck in his skin. He jumped up and saw columns of them marching up and down the tree trunk and up his jacket tail.

— Aw bl'd 'n sand me colonial f'kin oath.

When I got there he was dancing round the lorry

park in his underpants. Passers-by were laughing and lamenting, going aiyee and yoyoyo and ock-ock-ock. One of them helped Wesley pick off the ants.

— You see, he said. They are guarding the tree from us. It is why we are calling them *askari* ants. You with this bananas in your pocket, it did this.

Wesley had just got his shirt on when a grey Fiat lorry pulled in. It had a Dar es Salaam box number on its doors, Kaduva KP Exporting Import on its second trailer canvas. Two Somalis in their Muslim *kanzus* jumped out the cab, one of them unloading a primus from the cubby. Wesley was still scraping the bananas from his pocket so I walked over to the lorry. The Somali pumping the stove said:

— Two hours, *mbili*, after police coming.

— Two, I said pointing at Wesley. *Mbili, mimi wa mwenzi?* Juba, *ndio?*

— *Ndiyo ndiyo.* He was impatient and threw his arms out. *Saa mbili.*

Wesley came over and I told him we were going to Juba in two hours. He said he didn't like this Gulu town. I said neither did I so it better not rain because one deluge would cut us off.

We went back over to the New Suitable, seeing as it might be the last coffee we'd drink for days. Wesley said the ants had stripped him like a whittlin stick. Ebrahim said the coffee was finished, so I sat at a table on the verandah outside while Wesley went off looking for a stick to pick his teeth with. A white Land Rover pulled up and a soldier looked at me with his elbow on the window trim. He got out with the engine running and slammed the door.

— Hey you.

I looked up. He was just another gum-chewing soldier, Special Force uniform, mirror shades under cocked bush hat, cracked lips white with sun block or glucose powder.

— You have benzine? Petro?

— What's benzine? I said. No, I've nothing.

He was furious, a snake cut in half.

— MY BENZINE! he raved at me, arms twitching, neck popping. He spat his gum in the dirt and almost went to pick it up but unwrapped another stick like a tranquilliser and curled it into his mouth. It didn't work, he was still mad, jerking his thumb at a UN truck in the bus park.

— You no drive truck?

I shook my head. The soldier stared a moment then shoved himself back in the Land Rover and swung wide into the middle of the road snarling gears. Wesley came back with his tooth stick.

— Ay oop. Wha's wi'im, soldier ants?

— Thinks I've got his benzine in my lorry.

— Caw, kickin' up Bob's-a-dyin were'n 'e. Don't like it at all, this Gulu. Too fulla chocolate sodjers. See y'up lorry park youth. Bess keep an eye on our two mud-pilots.

— You think it's gonna rain then?

— Aye, maybe. They're restless under mango city anyroad.

Half an hour later a man stopped beside me.

— What are you doing please?

He wasn't polite, or angry, he just had that cold, implacable, still voice of a hunter. I thought through

182

my next move before looking up. I'd been stupid, sitting there in full view, making a picture postcard showing the broken flagpole, the boarded-up Caltex Station, a pitted road and bullet-hole walls. Joke captions too: BIRTHPLACE OF OBOTE. SOLDIER GUZZLING BENZINE. WELCOME TO GULU WELLS . . .

There were three of them, two standing in the road below looking up, the sharp one astride the empty chair at my table. All three wore raincoats and dark glasses. Spycatcher had a black attaché case with leopard-skin edging.

— Where from? Europe? he said.

I looked at the other two. One of them had tiny ears and tennis shoes with red toe caps. I was about to answer when Spycatcher stood and jumped down.

— Come with us. He beat the dust off his black nylon trousers. We are from Intelligence. Military Police. Come now. It is best.

No laughs in that. Just because they dressed out the rag bag for Uganda that your granny sent to the Scouts didn't mean they weren't Intelligentsia. There were tribal hack marks down Spycatcher's temples. He was a mackerel-back Nilotic, an Acholi insider, probably killed his brother to get there. The other two were cousins, maybe.

— Give me this book please.

— What book? I said, like an amateur crook, giving the game away instead of just handing it over and saying: oh thanks, I thought you might be interested in my work, it's for sale if you'd like to buy it . . . I'll tell you what, you keep it and have twenty Sportsman too . . .

— This, papers. Give me.

He came forward as I went to jump down. There was still a chance they were just posturing on their way to check a few Chinese dishes and combs on the Somali lorry. Tennis Shoes blocked my jump and pointed to the steps a few yards along.

— Please, use this to come down.

It was this politeness which scared me most. As I touched down, the tall one came forward and took my notebook. We set off towards the lorry park, the notebook read as we went along.

Wesley was squatting on his heels in the shade.

— *Jambo* gentlemen, he said. Customs?

I shook my head at him, trying to look like a warning, a big frown to exaggerate gravity.

— Five 'ndred bob a-piece youth, he said. Juba by *boukrah*. T'morrer mornin.

— Subject to critic's choice, I said, drawing his attention to the tall one who took my notebook under the shade of a tree. He squatted, flicking through the pages like a card sharp while the other two searched the Somali lorry.

— Nay fret, Wesley said. 'S only a customs check, *magendo* like, checkin-checkin.

The two Somalis were unmoved too. Squatting over their tea and chapattis in the thin strip of shade along the lorry's edge. Wesley sat on his camel bag after elaborate scrutiny of the ground, the air, the branch above him.

— It's my notebook, I said.

— Oh, geddit. Don't bake yer spuds, youth, these lead soldiers're cunnin as deaf pigs.

184

I'm sure Wesley would've been your ideal gunner in the Ypres Salient, a right cheery Tommy in the mud, but he was getting on my tits now. One glum remark, one glimmer of pessimism might've saved the day.

— Hey, pssstttt-psssttt. The Intelligence one under the tree was making spidery motions with his hand. *Mzungu*. What is this writing say? Who is these soldiers, eh? Here, you say: *the police are beating* . . . what is this wud? *the fuck?* Fuck? What police? This is today!

— It's nothing, I said.

— No, you say this: *the police are beating the fuck* . . . Eh? Yes, it say the fuck out of some poor Acholi son of Obote . . . This ayee verra verra bad. President Obote is Langi. He is not with Acholi son. The police do not beat Acholi. What is it to mean? You say what, *mwingereza?*

— It says luck, not fuck. I am a Christian. I do not use this word. It means they are beating the luck, you know, bad luck. He did wrong. No luck. He get caught, so the police punish him for doing wrong . . .

— Why you write this book, eh?

— It's not a book.

Wesley stood between us and thumped his camel bag on the cinders.

— *Jambo* sir. Any trouble?

The Acholi closed my notebook and opened his case. I leaned as far forward as I dared to see inside. Pair of scissors, some green foolscap and a cheap hand mirror with a green plastic frame. Scissors no doubt for cutting stencil codes and the mirror for signals. The case snapped shut. He glared at Wesley, eyes like two barrels of a sawn-off shotgun. Wesley didn't seem perturbed.

— *Mzuri*. We go now? he said. There is no trouble pal. This man has done nothing wrong. I am a teacher at Mbugazali College with Father Grimble who is a friend of President Milton His Excellency Apollo Obote. Listen, the President's son is in my History S4 . . .

— You're joking? I said, too astonished to stay cautious. You teach for Grimble? But the Acholi rounded on Wesley.

— You shut also English. Do not talk to me! You are a journalist too eh? We watchid you in first, two, three days, yes. In Gulu there is come three journalist. You looking here, you looking there. You say you are a titcher, eh? All titcher are journalist. Writing the books with lies and bad things of Uganda. Show me inside this.

He pointed at Wesley's camel bag. Wesley suddenly looked like the bloke sure to have a fuckin typewriter in his bag. Well, I was halfway there. He had poems on blue airmail foolscap typed up ready to read to his mate Ivan in Sudan over coffee and fags. The Acholi confiscated them.

— That's me oop spout, down mine, youth.

— They belong to me, I said to the Acholi. I wrote them. He was looking after them for me.

Wesley shook his head.

— No no, he said. I wrote them. Crackin good stuff some of it. Me *Charcoal Trilogy*.

— Lies, the Acholi said.

186

I was beginning to like this Acholi. He might give Wesley some much needed constructive crit.

— Sorry mate, I said to Wesley. Look, I said to the Acholi. I do not know this man. I never saw him before today. Let him go on the lorry. He is a teacher for Father Grimble.

The Acholi ignored me and just made noises: *Eir Eir*, calling the other two over: *pss pss, tell them to go, drive*. He waved his hand at the Somalis, dismissing them. *You are cleared, go!*

I whispered to Wesley to just get on the lorry. Ignore the Acholi. From Juba telephone the BBC Monitoring Unit in Kenya, memorise the number . . . But Wesley was being that Tommy, that stoical Christian from *Pilgrim's Progress*.

— 'S okay man, just leave it to some angel's oil.
— What is he say!
— He says nothing.
— You make lies eh?
— No.
— He is coming this *mzungu*. Your friend.
— He is not my friend.
— No. You one. You two. Where is the three?
— There are none.
— Where are you sleep? *Hoteli?* Why you no at Missions or Acholi Inn?

My rucksack was in Daniel's quarters for safe-keeping but now I could see them dragging Daniel off too.

— Over the road, New Suitable, Wesley said, thumbing behind him.
— Lying.

The other two Acholis were still at loose ends beside the squatting Somalis. There'd been an argument and one of the Somalis was holding up his hand which dripped spaghetti and tomato sauce, making signals in the air and shrugging. He licked his fingers.

— You authority, he said to the Acholi. You must sign chit, paper, custom goodies. For us drive, you sign.

I tried once more too.

— We must leave Gulu, I said. People are waiting for us. We are late. Easter is finished, they are worried. They hear nothing. They know we are in Gulu. We are going on this lorry . . .

— No, you stay!

The one with the red toe caps said:

— Hey Ojwong, they say you must sign them. He held up a clipboard so Ojwong went over and signed the Somalis clear but shouted at them and dug in his pockets. He ferretted down the lining and pulled out his beret, unfurled it, beat the fluff off and put it on.

— Nine bob square, Wesley said.

Ojwong came back, briefcase under his wing, mouth gathering a clot. Wesley went forward to meet him, digging just as deep in his own lining.

— Suppose we like, pay you for your trouble, eh? Time is money. Thirsty is work. Beer, *malwa, chai*, we buy, eh?

Ojwong spat, pulled his beret down and stood like a cadet.

— No. You come, you-you.

— Please, I said. Let this man go to Juba. We

are not friends. I do not know him. He travels. I travel different. He is not a brother . . .

— Finish, *ninyi*. Somali, *dereva* go now! Ojwong waved his hands like the Somalis were sweat bees.

— No *peksen?* the driver said. He was unrolling a prayer mat and the other washed his hands from a yellow jug.

— Finish, *kwisha. Kwenda.*

Red Toes said:

— Do as he orders. Do your prayings at Bungatira.

— Fuck, I said to Wesley. I really am sorry.

— Ah cummon youth, no needs. We'll juss tek our Daniel on nex' clipper.

— Jesus, don't mention that name . . .

— Ha, the third Acholi said. You think we are stupid. Listen to the good friends talk.

The Somalis rolled up their prayer mats and packed their mess away. The mate beckoned Wesley to get in the cab.

— No man, he said. Impossible. *Boukrah, inshallah.*

— *Inshallah,* they said, unrolling the prayer mats again as we were motioned to move off behind the two subordinates. Ojwong walked behind us, calling hey, and showing us a pistol when we turned to look, like a watch-seller in a market.

At the crossroads we were ordered to stop.

— Where is your friend, eh? Hey you, with this face like Kenya *jok,* like Bob Marley. He was pulling imaginary hairs on his chin and looking at Wesley. This *mzungu,* where? This? This? He pointed three ways.

189

— Caw, Wesley said. You're givin me the pip. Who's 'e talkin about?

Ojwong wouldn't give up.

— Eh, yes, Stanley Road, where?

— Listen pal, I don't know. *Hapana mzungu.*

— He doesn't know, I said. I don't know. We do not travel together. We are all alone, one-one . . .

It was hot and close and there were flies all over our shoes. We heard the Somali lorry start up like an old bomber in the distance. We walked on, followed by children. A crested crane swooped across the road throwing a shadow like sheets on a line.

I shoved my hands in my pockets, feeling loose notes in my sweaty palms and a small pocket notebook with a pink cover. It was just cheap from an Asian *duka* near Austen's but it was bloody near full too with tiny writing, all those things that would get Ojwong a Mercedes from the commander.

All five of us flagged uphill. Wesley puffed and bladdered, saying he was used to fags at 'alf time, but this was torture under the Geneva Convention. We were walking behind some women on their way home from market with empty baskets, the girls carrying gourds.

— Hello sir, how are you? they said.

— Knackered, Wesley said. Knackered *mkubwa mzuri.*

The girls giggled, the women said aii heh. Ojwong said something in their language and the women spoke back sharply but with their heads bowed.

The police station building was set behind a tall

hedge, one storey, green *mabati* roof, grey walls and peeling plaster. It was half covered in vine and shaded by frangipani and a tamarind set well back in the long grass behind the outbuildings and thorn bushes. Two sunbirds flashed across the doorway. I watched the geckos on a sunny patch of wall till Ojwong pushed me into the cool dry interior. I looked around for the bicycle inner tube cabinet.

The duty sergeant was jolly and, for a second, I thought he'd dismiss the Acholis when he saw them and, I don't know, call them naughty boys like friendly coppers do.

— Hello sir, and to you sir, what is the problem? The lorry, it is gone. You did not have a ride?

Then he saw Ojwong and his face smoothed out. Ojwong came forward and nubbed his finger several times on the open chargebook.

— Nems! he said. All your nems. Bookid.

The duty sergeant looked embarrassed because he loved the British, he was almost a British police-man, we were all white men, but he couldn't spell our names so we wrote them ourselves. Wesley Scaife. N. H. Tickner. Ojwong wanted more. Age, address, thumb-print. Then he lifted my hat.

— Tek off your wig!

— It isn't a wig.

— What is it? What is that?

— Ponytail. Fringe.

— Ach, he said. You think you are from Watutsi?

A boy PC in a second-hand faded blue uniform escorted us into a corridor out back. A man in shorts and bare feet was sweeping dead insects, safari ants and beetle shucks with a grass broom along the walls and out into the same corridor. Ojwong and his recruits had gone ahead through a green door. I looked at the sweeper and recognised the man who'd been beaten with the inner tube.

— *Jambo bwana*, he said.

He radiated happiness and danced round us with his broom.

— Soldier ants bin through, youth, Wesley said. Sin 'em eat a frog in five minutes, cor! 'side from me.

The recruits came back without Ojwong. They said they were going to find our other friend, and then there'd be trouble for all three of us. They'd left the door half open. We could hear voices like bongo drums, then the door was closed and a shiny faced young guard came out in his faint grey uniform, so neat, he was smiling and stood to attention.

— Who's in there? I asked him.

— Theeee boss, he said. He leaned his rifle against the wall.

— What do they say?

— Ah, these intelligence ones, they are very stupid rilly. They saying you can be spies.

— Caw bl'd 'n sand. Fag mate? Wesley offered him a *Guardian Weekly*. I gave him a Sportsman.

— Are they policemen?

— They are not policee-men. One day they come in Mercedes from Kampala and live in the barracks. This one is Acholi, put in by Vice-President Muwanga. This is what they say.

By now my guts were taking it worse than my

head. My hands were drubbing flecks of notebook inside my pocket and they were sticking like dough to my fingers. I asked if I could go to the toilet.

— It is there, the guard said, pointing down past the cells to a shed. But you must wait. Hey Paitoo, tek this man to the water close-it.

Paitoo carried a herdsman's stick and asked if I was ill. I rubbed my stomach.

— *Kuhara*, I said. The runs.

— Oh, sorry, he said.

Paitoo stood with the door open.

— Regulations, he said.

I took my jacket off and pulled down my trousers. Paitoo turned away and kept just out of vision. No white man ever showed an African his body in pride. Shrivelled up white chicken flesh, maggoty-cocked, pimply and heat rashed. Poor Paitoo, his colonial hankering of better days destroyed at the door of the *choo*. I made a few sloppy farts with my mouth to add veracity and to cover the rustling of my notebook. I just hoped Paitoo wasn't a detective, or worse, a stool pigeon with an eye for distinguishing evidence. I pulled my trousers up, climbed on to the toilet, praying it was secure on its concrete base, and looked through the open window. The backyard, tall dry grass and thorn bushes. I dropped the notebook and the last few postcards down the wall and into the grass.

The boss was waiting for us, so the guard showed us in and shut the door. It was a dark room with a big black safe and a slow ceiling fan creaking over a desk. The boss was Chief Superintendent Musoke. He was built like a weight-lifter and wedged behind the desk. He sweated rings like truck wheels under his armpits. A rush mat was nailed across the window behind him to make a blind. Ojwong stood beside him looking bloodthirsty. The Chief looked anxious, his small pink-edged lips flickering as he spoke. He slapped the back of his moist neck.

— Good afternoon. How are you?

Ojwong grunted and shifted, so the Chief amended the greeting.

— Give me your passports please.

Ojwong snatched them from the Chief's hand and sprung through the stiff pages then threw them onto the desk like a busted flush. The Chief was gentler, his fingers feeling over the details.

— What are you doing here, eh Sciff . . . what is this name?

— Scaife. The name's Wesley Scaife.

— Weazly. Uhmm. Okay Mr Weazly, what are you doing in Gulu? Vacation?

— I'm a teacher at Mbugazali College. I'm travelling to Juba to visit friends . . .

Ojwong picked up my passport.

— Who are you? he shouted. No-man, eh? Says titcher. Where do you think you titch?

— Allow me to see this, the Chief said. Ah yes, No-man. You are a titcher also? Where?

— Nairobi.

— Yes, very good.

My confiscated notebook was on the desk and the Chief's fingers descended towards it like he was

194

making a little parachute man to make the kids laugh. He was playing for time, reluctant and perplexed. His fingers drummed across the book. It wasn't an entirely unconscious action because he modulated the drumming to fit the rhythm of his question.

— So . . . drum . . . what . . . drum-drum . . . is . . . this about . . . drum-drum-drum . . . this book?

Ojwong was chewing a twig, sucking it dry. The Chief started picking the corners of his old blotter. There was a nice little rock he used as a paperweight. It tilted so he picked it up and twisted it, rocked it, inverted it. The flies jumped from one finger to the next like stepping stones. The fan slowed, but never quite stopped, then sped up. It was sticking on every other revolution. Smack. The Chief's hand on the back of his neck again. And the dry lap and rasp of Ojwong's tongue like filthy water on the harbour wall, calm oily water in the hot afternoon.

— It's private, I said. It's for me. I want to remember my travels in Africa. I want to read it to my grandchildren . . .

— No, Ojwong said, as contemptuous of the Chief's leniency as he was of my lies. It is false journalist lies.

He snatched it off the desk and turned the pages till he found today and pointed for the Chief to read. He read aloud.

— *Sodjer in Land Rover angry like snake cut in half ask me for his benzine, UN magendo supply to army?* This man, the Chief pointed to Ojwong, he says there is no soldier. He says he watchid you writing this without any soldier. This is a problem, my friend.

195

Yes . . . He read more: *Gulu is like a termites' nest with the top lopped off, soldiers run everywhere . . . all Easter nothing but stolen aid comes to Gulu to feed the army* . . . You see, this is very very bad that you should write this. Why do your grandchildren want to know it for? Oh, and why do you think President Obote is in this man's tribe? He is not Acholi. I am very sorry for this.

The Chief was genuinely upset about it. He even put his cap on like a judge passing sentence.

— I don't know what to do with you.

It was obviously time to plead before we heard any tommy-rot from Wesley who was rubbing his guts. Maybe he was jealous his poems hadn't been read out yet.

— Listen, I said. There was a man, in a Land Rover. He said these things. He was drunk. I've waited for a lorry for five days. Five days! What is there to do? I sit and wait and write in my diary . . . If I was a journalist, I'd know that President Obote was not Acholi. Yes?

This was underarm bowling. Wesley must've felt national shame or Nottingham pride because he chose right now to reveal his medical condition. One belch like a crowbar on a nail and the room was hit by rotton egg.

— Aye oop, he said. Got giardia. School beans. 'Alf the kids in school've got it.

The Chief heaved himself up and fanned his nose with our passports. He took a bunch of keys from his pocket, unlocked the safe and slipped our passports into a little drawer. I could've said bravo

Wesley. He could've said southern git. It was neck-and-neck so far. Wesley's turn:

— Aw cummon Chief. All travellers keep diaries and write postcards, you know that. Why all this checkin-checkin? Why lock our passports here?

— They are safe here. You are safe here. You do not understand. We are protecting you from, let us say, some elements. It is very dangerous to travel today. Let us call it operations. If you are seen today near these operations, there are some criminal elements who still think this way: the time when two Germany men, uh? writing-writing postcards, this and that, things about army and whatnot. There is no police chief like me to help them. I did not control these men. They took these Germanies to the barracks and I am sorry. Eh? They shote them.

The fan had stopped. Ojwong was fiddling with the switch and Wesley's gut-gas was hurrying the proceedings.

— It is broken, Ojwong said.

— No, the electricity is over.

— Tch. Ojwong spat all over Wesley's face. This place. It will not do enough things. Huh. I will die here.

The Chief picked up Wesley's blue foolscap.

— Me *Charcoal Trilogy*, Wesley said.

— What is this?

— Poetry.

Go on Chief, I thought, burn our ears with some charcoal. Wesley was almost rubbing his hands. The Chief shuffled through the pages. Wesley stepped forward.

— No no, Chief, dun't make sense that way. It's a sequential trilogy, like process of makin charcoal – from the tree to a brew, ged it?

— Eh? Is it nonesense?

— It's lies, Ojwong said. Look, it is type writing. He is makin newspaper. Give me.

He left the Chief with two pages and they both started to read simultaneously.

— *Sargeant . . . Benson's baw . . . dy basket battalian slants of moon in rifle's range ricochets . . .*

— *Full si . . . newed you struggle sunwards lionlunged in dawn's drumbeats . . .* Uhmmmm, the Chief said. It will need to be examined.

— It is in code, Ojwong said. You are finished, my friend.

— Tomorrow I am coming, at nine o'clock, the Chief said. There will be investigation.

The notebook and *Charcoal Trilogy* went into Ojwong's case.

— Ay oop, where's me royalties? Wesley said. You read the Geneva Convention, man.

— You must stay here, for protection. It is a case.

— You can't keep us here for nothing.

— Oh it is nothing eh? Ojwong said. If you are guilty, we can know.

The Chief smiled, maybe he found it funny.

— You must not worry, please. Relax here. We can find out today. You are Breetsh, haha, yes. Goodbye.

NINETEEN

I turned into Le Haut Bois at five o'clock on a warm June afternoon driving a white Rancho. I'd bought it off the street in Brighton, my vehicle to a new life: £150 ono, 1 week tax, 3 weeks MOT, needs tidying.

As soon as I pulled into the yard I could see something was wrong. I'd only been gone seven days, but the sudden height of the weeds made it look like a year later. The tomato plants were fat bushes now, and the potatoes were stretching the fence round the dung heap. The Land Rover sat like a wreck in a scrapyard. There was only one goose, his feathers split, widower's face, eyes wiped blank with a brillo pad. This was the goose you couldn't approach before. His name was Pois Chiche, chick pea, a pun on the French for goose, *oie*. He'd torn and ripped my clothes countless times and chased me up a pear tree twice. Once, I grabbed a broom stick and that goose smacked it with a shoulder wing bone and snapped it in two. He ate metal, and had a split foot from a previous encounter with a vixen. He was the defender of the pack, the yard's force field. Now he just looked up at the strange car which he'd normally have leapt on, pulled off the loose plastic and trapped the driver inside. Just looked up and went back to staring at the grass.

I thought most people returned home with relief, a sense of nothing changed, the stable home. At Le Haut Bois we never did. After a barn had collapsed, after Aunay's intrusions, we always turned the corner in anticipation. What next? Who's been? What's dead? What's fallen off, rotted, deteriorated or run away?

The pitiful state of the lone goose betrayed the whole event. I found ducks' feet scattered round the pond, a rotting carcass upside down by the yellow irises and chicken feathers like blossom in the trees. In the cowshed was another goose, Haut Bois, sitting on his feet, neck curled on the ground. He must've died in his sleep, or of starvation, or shock, squeezing himself under the door in a panic during the fight as the fox tore his friends apart and Pois Chiche put up the only struggle. I turned Haut Bois over and cascades of maggots wriggled down, fat and yellow. As I wailed in anger Pois Chiche thought he heard his mate and came rushing over, all hope revived. He saw a dead lump and started wailing too, so I led him away like a child, put the dead Haut Bois in a black sack and collected the duck ends on a shovel.

I followed the flattened grass tracks through the field. They criss-crossed, and where they met there were patches where the fox had stopped and bitten through another foot. The crows and buzzards had picked them clean but I still recognised them from the feathers. There was Schick by the pond upside down, Austen by the apple tree, his cowlick feather still sticking out. And poor old Wesley who I thought might've tried flying.

I followed the tracks as far as the barbed wire fences to see if I could find any hair or fur. There were grey dry hairs on all six crossing points. This was a dog, a small hard-skinned dog too. I went back to the maze of trails and examined the flat spots which I'd assumed were made by a stalking or eating fox. There was a piece of shit with a boot print. It was nothing like mine. A dog and a person had been in the field. I felt disappointment more than anything. I couldn't pin that down.

From the distance, the far end of the long field, I could hear piano-playing coming from a barn. There were eighteen pianos in that barn, all belonging to a concert pianist from Paris who jumped from one to the other, stamping out Mozart minuets, Chopin waltzes, Beethoven sonatas. I'd seen the man once, walking back from the station after a European tour to promote his latest CD of moonlight favourites. Unshaven, grubby shirt, grey stubble like a wild boar, his playing tails sticking out of a plastic bag. His mother and girlfriend had left him, run off together back to Paris. He refused to shake hands with farmers because he said they'd crush his fingers. He kept a pack of wolf-dogs in an outdoor cage. His twenty peacocks wandered homeless over the fields. I found one roosting in my apple tree once. Every year the fox slaughtered them all but he just replaced them.

That night I stood in the lane and heard the pianist playing in a full moon, tinkling at first like a man tiptoeing through his barn, eighteen sleeping pianos. Then a sudden anger and madness and he's jumping from one to the next and they're roaring

like he'd woken the beasts. The dogs howled anyway, and it was the snarling of those tanks cursing
through the orchards. Then Juliette was standing
beside me saying run, run into the fields with me.

TWENTY

Me and Wesley were standing with the guard when Ojwong's boys came in with this white woman. The Chief opened his door, his brown shoes squeaked and he held a shopping bag made of crocodile skin. He was as surprised as us to see her there, and you could tell he just wanted to go home and forget the mess Ojwong had made for him.

— Ah, he said to me, here is your friend. You, he said to the woman, you are the missionary in Atiak? Why are you involved here?

She untucked her mouth and looked at me, floppy white sunhat, sandle straps, shrugging open her jacket with hands still in the pockets.

— I'm not involved and I'm not his friend, she said. And I am not a goddam missionary any more.

— Tomorrow, the Chief said, I am coming at nine. You must wait here now, I cannot let you free in Gulu. You are safe here tonight.

— What do you mean safe? the woman said. I don't even know these people.

— Atiak, I said. Joy, you're Joy from Atiak?

— So what does that make you? Mr Stanley?

— Yeah, I said, if you're that constipated it does.

Or do I just wish I'd said that? Because, and it can't be denied, we'd arrived at this meeting we both wished had never taken place. For me it was an anti-climax which exposed every false note I'd ever played in Africa. And, when it comes to it, do I even remember what was really said? Not likely. It's a contradiction, but I never felt it was an encounter which changed my life either. I had no life to change. If anything, it was a meeting between one young man who'd found nothing to believe in, and a young woman about to demolish everything she'd ever believed in. This leaves no room for distinction. The only species to emerge is singular and self-devouring. Two survivors fighting over a life-belt.

It was unjust I know, but I felt deceived by Joy. I was angry with my imagination too, for sanctifying someone I was never going to like. An imagination which had more or less turned this gold-panning missionary into an alchemist of the soul. The same imagination which, now angry, became perverse and said: here's the woman you're going to marry anyway, whether you like it or not.

Ojwong wasn't fooled by our meeting.

— Spies lies, he said, you are well known friends.

— They think we're spies, I said.

— Well maybe you are, Joy said. She stared at the long parched grass, refusing to look at any of us. Ojwong tried pincing his fingers on to her elbow.

— Yes, take her away, I said.

— Move out, he said, I know about you, I'm from around. But she shrugged him off and he started rooting in his pocket for the pistol.

— I mean, she said to me, just what are you *doing* in Africa, you bum?

She always said, throughout our time together, that when I walked into her life she'd been about to jump, okay, but I'd gone and pushed her instead. And I said no, I was already walking out of her life when she walked into mine.

After sunset the guardroom turned cool. There was no electricity, just moonlight and paraffin. The young constable stood out back under a porch and the roof banged and clanked as it cooled. Now and then a dust-devil swept across the compound. Maybe two hours passed before the duty sergeant tried being hospitable and brought Joy in to join us. She didn't object. He said we could sit or 'walk on our legs', and if we wanted anything he could send a boy to fetch it.

— Three strong teas, I said.

— Aye, and a chip cob, Wesley said, stretching out for a kip in his doss bag. He took his teeth out and put them on the floor beside a lighted candle stub. As soon as the first snore ganged up his nose Joy said:

— Well? You didn't answer my question.

I said her question was flawed, that it shouldn't just address me but *all* of us in white undercoat. And, maybe to simplify the answer, we should just take our God and our Blue Peter clothes and leave Africa alone.

I knew my argument was incoherent, even if it gathered logic in my mind as it rolled. I'd never voiced it before, or I'd simply never had one. What-ever, I'd kept it to myself till Joy set it in motion,

205

like all this time we'd been two explorers on collision course. Or, if I'd deliberately sought her out, she got my own question in first: *what am I doing in Africa?*

Now, given the chance to discover why, I was confused by anger. I said things like I dreamed of the day when maybe I could forget Africa, or at most, years hence, recall some hazy notion of what it had been like there in the post-colonial days, years after every white face had been thrown onto an aeroplane. I said I dreamed too of the day when every African would burn a Bible alongside an effigy of a Catholic priest. Me, I'd be thousands of miles away in a log cabin with some fishing gear, smelling the cool fresh water and saying sorry man, it won't happen again.

— How so? she said.

I didn't know. I was just remembering this kid at Lake Baringo back in Kenya. One morning I'd walked into the village with a fisherman and his 7-year-old boy ran out to greet us. He looked at me then asked his father: *has this man been saved by the blood of Christ?* The fisherman said yes, then told me that his son wouldn't speak to me unless I had been. So, what did Joy think of that?

— You've got all the wrong answers, she said, but none of the right questions.

— Really? I said. Well here's a good question for *you*. What do you mean you're not a missionary any more?

There was killing in the distance. We stopped to listen. It was in the scrub round Gulu but moving away, bursts of gunfire every few seconds. A nightjar spooked by the window. A pinked moon lit up a white UN Land Rover as it ghosted in, headlights off. An armed soldier and two policemen slipped from the shadows on the forecourt. They off-loaded drums of petrol, sacks of rice and a barrel of cooking oil. Another Land Rover started up and backed into view, its back door flung open. UGANDA POLICE. Stencilled in red on the blue panels: A GIFT FROM THE EEC. The driver in the UN truck waited, white arm crooked over the window channel. The glow of an unhurried cigarette. Another *mzungu* stood there as the police vehicle drove away. A voice said:

— Okey-dokey. Let's skid.

The truck started up. One of the men laughed. Wesley woke and came over to the window.

— Fuckim Ovviv, he said with his gums.

The cigarette was tossed down like a spent firework. The soldier picked it up and emptied it in two long drags. The truck set off without lights. The African silence, just a soldier's boots on the gravel, nose-blowing with fingers. Mosquitoes, crickets. Prisoners groaning in their sleep across the yard, coughing, hawking. In a few hours I'd have to lie again, lie faster than a dog licks a dish.

— Come on then Stanley, give me my marching orders, Joy said. Describe the sin. Why is my God a white elephant? You want me gone, so tell me why.

— What do you want, emergency theology?

— You're not up to it Stanley. But you've been around some. You must have a story to tell. You get me arrested as your accomplice, so bumming through Africa must mean something or you wouldn't be such a flirt with the truth. Who's your problem? *Magendo?* The White Fathers? Saint Kizito? Christian Aid?

— Yeah, I said, as a matter of fact all of them.

— Then tell me about it Stanley. I want to know. Tell me why I shouldn't go work for Christian Aid.

— 'Cause they're arseholes, Wesley said, slotting his teeth in just for the occasion.

— You keep out of this, Joy said. I want to hear from Stanley.

She was right, I wasn't up to it. If I pushed her it was an accident. Wesley was half-conscious so I said:

— You tell her. You work for Grimble.

— Man's a hierophant, youth. Arsehole in a dog collar. Punches boys 'steada Bibles.

Joy was disbelieving.

— You do not work for Father Grimble.

— Aye lass, I do. History man.

— What's he got to do with Christian Aid, Stanley? she said.

— Bl'd an' sand, Wesley said, what's the man got to do with Christian anything? Pisses charity up wall, threatens to shoot my cat with a crossbow.

— Uganda respects him, Joy said.

— Aye, respect him or be damned. Lass, the man could've taken over from Amin. Bit o' *matoke* up his jumper an' some boot polish. But you can't shift him. Water won't wash grease away. I've even bin t'Pope's Nuncio 'bout the man. Dah, won't touch 'im will they.

208

— He's one man, Joy said. I want to know about Christian Aid, Stanley. You're the spy. Tell me about them.

I told her about a week I'd spent in Karamoja at the International Christian Aid base camp. A knock-up village with an airstrip, solid bungalows round a massive supplies hangar. There were Dodge pick-ups parked on the drives outside the bungalows, flower tubs and yellow T-shirts hanging on the line to dry. This was Faminesville, Wyoming.

A mile away; there were 30,000 Karamajong villagers hiding from the army in an extinct volcano living on wild berries and insects, dying of malaria and dysentry. The cattle were gone. The only thing on all fours were pissed Christian Aid workers. They spent their days pottering around the void just to use up gasoline. Attempts to reach the refugees were blocked by soldiers. If the refugees came down, they were shot. Work was all on stand-by. Faminesville was like an American private school in vacation time, a few teachers stay on just to use the pool on their own. You walk round the dead buildings with the sun in your ear chewing Beef Jerkeys and inventing your life.

There was one married couple, Chuck and Sam. I sat with them one evening drinking Kentucky bourbon and eating potato chips from Seattle. Chuck was the mechanic and Sam the nurse, both from below the American Bible Belt. Chuck wore over-sized dungarees, long black beard and round specs. Sam was made of pipe cleaners and adenoids. The potato chips were stale and there were another thousand jumbo-size packets to get through. They told me about the battle, the day the gunships attacked Namalu and cornered some bandits, a whole day of shelling but only two bullets went through the Christian Aid compound. Chuck said they thanked the Lord. Sam said amen and Chuck reached under the chair and pulled out the calf skin. It was Gospel and chips night. Chuck went all 'we-wanna-share-the-Lord-with-you'. Sam said:

— Have you thought about saving yourself from hell?

— Yay Norman, yay, Chuck said. I'm afraid you're headin' to hell, verily man.

— How do you know that? I said. I aint told anyone yet.

— Forgive me for saying it Norm, but you're on an ego-trip.

Just so I'd know what was in store for me, they described my destination. Hell was a nine-mile cube where I'd live life as I'd done on earth, but because of the congestion with other un-saved ones, I'd be frustrated from carrying out my tasks. How did they know?

— Because you're in hell, I said.

No, it was in Revelations. They were prepared to give up their evenings to help me study the Gospels.

Every evening the men congealed round several long tables put end to end in the warehouse. It was beer-can boredom. There was arm wrestling, can crushing in the fist, and the best game of all: piling the cans, one on top of the other, till they made a twenty-foot pillar from the table top up to the roof beam where they wedged and held. So far they'd managed four pillars of wisdom.

A plane came three times a week. There was a fleet of nine parked up in Nairobi at the Wilson airport. Cessnas, Beechcraft, Pipers. California dreaming, logos and livery, from four to twenty seaters. The mechanic said all the rich old wrinkly widows from the Bible Belt gave ICA so much leg-up they had to spend it on something, so they bought airplanes which then sat idle in their hangars if they didn't fly out to Namalu three times a week just to take the rubbish on Wednesdays, the empties on Thursdays and to bring the newspapers, puzzle books and sci-fi novels on Mondays. I went out with the empties.

— Out with the empties, Joy said when I'd finished. Maybe that's the story of your life. You're an unlucky explorer, Stanley.

— Missionaries have all the luck do they? I said.

— I'm not a goddammed missionary.

— So you said. Were you ever?

— If you want to know, in my room at school I had this colour picture from the *National Geographic* pinned on the wall. A missionary family making their way up the Zambezi in a dug-out canoe powered by an outboard motor. The clean young man and his wife, earnest Americans. He wore a pink sports shirt and she a yellow dress with a straw hat. His shirt was so well ironed and he sat in the prow looking upriver, jaw like the bowsprit as his wife's blonde hair was lifted by the breeze and her eyes gazed along the banks in wonder. She was like the Lady of Shalott to me. I was fifteen. Two beautiful white children with blonde hair sat with their backs to the missionaries. An African manned the outboard, clutching the tiller. A Pentecostal guide in a grey bush jacket sat nearby, an African in wide rimmed spectacles. The boat was loaded with belongings, a box full of kids' toys, a lampshade on the top, an English dustbin, a bicycle, a big radio nestled in some bedding, a white china toilet in the crook of the bow. Either side, the thick green jungle pressed dark on the swirling brown water of the Zambezi. It was a family I wanted, not the burden of ministry. I wanted to take that goddammed toilet into the bush.

— So why didn't you?

— You don't have a father like mine.

— Don't I? Maybe you don't have a father like mine either.

But she had. In fact she held the answer after all, or what would become the answer. Just before Easter she'd set off to visit her father in Kampala. It was the end of the dry season. There was no food and the last crop of finger millet had been ruined by army worm. The grass had been burned to dust and the animals hunted out the district. Travelling was over and the marriages had taken place. These were still, hot days with high dry winds and half the Acholi in Joy's district were bad with infected eyes. The nights were cold and they burned fires till morning and spent the days filling in the cracks in their huts and closing the doors tight. Joy was sick too, eyes, stomach, aching legs, sick of it all.

At the post office in Atiak she found a letter from

her father. The village lorry pulled in outside the police post to load up for Gulu. Women with their mangoes and cassava, two *mubende* goats, stolen schoolbooks, rags and chickens. The men had pipes and carved daggers and some uncured skins.

Joy read the letter on the lorry. The dust and swaying made her feel ill, the letter ten times worse.

Dear Joyce, I was not pleased to receive your letter, and I must say you certainly do start it in a thoroughly disrespectful manner. I am not Jerry to you but your father, I am Reverend, and I am, lest you forget, your spiritual guide and superior. Your anxieties are not up for discussion over Easter, let me make that plain. They do not concern me, they concern the Lord and if you cannot place them in His hands then I am afraid you are lost to me, as your sister Miranda was before you. I am afraid your mother never heeded me either . . .

In Gulu, Joy put up at the Safari Lodge but there was no transport to Kampala. She didn't want to stay with the sisters or the priests in Gulu, where she might've found a lift too. For all their dedication to poor Ugandans, they maintained a pure, clean, untouchable superiority which made her own achievements look so foolish. They were too suspicious of women's self-help groups and adult literacy. She was untouched by their smoothly operating light-giving God. Or by her father's 'read this tract or be damned' God.

She'd promised her father she'd do three years

in Acholiland and then he'd fund her next move anywhere in the world, even if it was with the money her mother had left her. But nothing she did was 'Christo-centric' enough. He cut her budget and was always saying she was just like her sister Miranda, the *mzungu* nun in Gulu who threw in the veil, renounced her vows and married an Asian shoe-seller in Nairobi. But Miranda was happy in her suburban redemption and Joy admired her resistance against their father.

Their father was the Reverend Cudlipp. He blamed the Italian doctors for corrupting his daughters. He said Miranda's decision was based on a heathen fairy-tale. It must've been the Italians. They lived sophisticated lives even in Gulu and were kind to missionaries. Even the Italian priests ate fresh spaghetti, white bread and home-made ice cream. They slept in beds with crisp cool white linen sheets and sunbathed in walled gardens full of hand-fed sunbirds, a swimming pool, guard dogs fed on carcasses. They grew grapes, for heaven's sake, and made wine. Miranda used to swim there, secretly. She'd always imagined California was like the Italian garden in Gulu.

Both sisters had been raised in Kampala, in one of those whitewashed brick houses on Kololo Hill where only the expatriate neighbours waxed their red cement floors, kept gardens ablaze in flamboyant trees and moonflower shrub and strolled arm in arm by the bandstand on Easter Monday. The Cudlipp family read the Bible aloud to one another while Gilbert & Sullivan and circling egrets floated on the hot air over Kampala and the happy strollers threaded their way between immaculately dressed Asians picnicking on the grass.

Joy had been raised by servants from the age of two. The houseboy and housegirl were orphans trained by priests. They'd slept on mats outside. The boy swept and slaved, the girl washed and scrubbed all day. The cook and her husband lived in a tin shed down the garden. Their failures were the only subjects of conversation at mealtimes. Boiled fish and mashed potatoes seven days a week. She'd never seen her mother so much as lift a pan in eighteen years. Living among black folk, she'd called it. Not her idea of heaven. What black folk? Four servants and a few Bible students in ecclesiastical shirts and black-rimmed spectacles who came to tea once a month. Civilised Bagandans who carried their prayer books to the john. When they'd left, wiping their feet before they went outside, Joy's father always sneered and said they might know their Gospels but they'd never learn to sip their tea properly. Joy had been ashamed of him for as long as she could remember.

She couldn't stay in Uganda, let alone Africa any longer. She'd written her father and said so. She was bookless and run-down, sleeping in a tin hut which baked in the heat, nothing but a rush mat on a dirt floor, an iron bed and a dirty grey sheet, while Miranda lived in a white suburb of Nairobi. Joy loved her yearly visit there, just to sit in the garden sipping juice with ice cubes and listening to the radio and the sound of the shower and the lawnmowers and the children's fluted accents. Miranda and

Sameer had three children at Hillcrest School. Every Christmas Miranda sent out dozens of copies of her Dear Folks round-robin family newsletter. Always saying the road to hell was paved with good intentions, that she really had decided to hand write six dozen personal letters, but life was too hectic, she just didn't have the time. The letters were always about the children. In school they were so clever that other mothers praised them on Speech Day. At sport they were selected for Combined Schools Rugby tour of Zimbabwe. On stage they were Best Junior Actors Interhouse Drama. Every visitor Miranda had over the year was given a paragraph: *they stayed for only one week but we took them on the train to Mombasa and it was a resounding success* . . . She described every visit to Treetops *(it was freezing cold, very misty and we hardly saw a thing!)*, every mating lion Natasha's friend Deborah saw and every baby her friends had, every fund-raising dinner and dance. But Joy's visits were described as *times of sombre reflection from my right-on spinster sister who only sees clean water once a year* . . . Joy's brother-in-law Sameer was in every paragraph: *Sameer has taken up shooting again. Sameer managed to get new import licences this year* . . . And people Joy didn't know called Pratish and Usha were *not too worried about going on long safaris, even after being messed about something shocking by Iberia* . . .

The Reverand Cudlipp wouldn't speak to Miranda again. He wasn't even a city missionary now, just a city man still bitter about Independence, a cold, devouring head of table. Back at Independence the Africans had said he wouldn't be needed.

Just see them get rid of me, he'd said. And when Amin had started his killing in Kampala, the Rev. Cudlipp had gone to the cathedral on his knees and quoted some prophet in the Bible: *if there be ten righteous men in the world* then stop the killing. That was useless. He ended up sitting on Amin's lap and giving him a kiss in front of the TV cameras.

She barely recalled her dead mother's face now, her smell or voice. Her father had stifled her mother like she was a leaking tap. There was always a closed door between them or a self-imposed silence. If she objected to anything, the Reverend said: *that's enough spite Nora. I bear the heartache of this house so I'll be the one to dish it up* . . . She wouldn't utter another word all day. Her father said: *when I speak, I change lives.* Her mother told Joy she'd never wanted to go to Africa at all, and if Joy had any sense she should quit the evil place the first chance she got.

— And you wouldn't come back? I said. If you quit?

— No, I won't come back.

— Yes you will, I said. I quit once, when I was fourteen. You remember the Marmite Kid?

— What are you saying, Stanley?

— Don't Stanley me any more. It was your father called me the Marmite Kid.

— You? Well that's great. That's all I need, someone more screwed up by Africa than me. What's the good of your advice?

— If you really wanna quit Africa, just hop on a lorry with me and Wesley tomorrow.

— I am not ready to run off with the Marmite Kid.

TWENTY-ONE

In the end me and Aunay had a fight. One afternoon in early July I was in the house when Aunay shouted through the doorway. He ordered me to move the Land Rover, he wanted to drive through to get water for his beasts. His tractor was parked on the lane with its wheels turned into the entrance, his daughter at the wheel. She was towing a water butt on the trailer. I said he hadn't the right, it was in the deeds: access to the *lavoir* with a wheelbarrow only. He called me something, either a cunt or a con-artist.

— My beasts are thirsty, he shouted. This is the farm of Madame Macé. Even under the Germans it was still a farm. Look what you've done. They've taken my fields . . .

I could see what I'd done. And yes, they'd taken his fields.

— I want water, Aunay said.

I knocked his straw hat off and it landed in the dirt. He goes: *awww, monsieur.* I called him an old bastard, Juliette's lover. He snorted like one of his beasts so I kicked the hat as he bent down to pick it up, kicked it down the path while his daughter sat watching from the tractor with a blank face. I'll always be ashamed, but I felt exhilaration because no one had ever stood up to him before. He was just a bully, an old man, trying to get his hat. I kicked it and kicked it and kicked it when really I should've thrown my arms round him and given Le Haut Bois back to him, out of respect for Madame Macé at least.

Retreat was the only option after that day, but I wanted to wait till 15 August. I wanted to see what the world might've been like on that day in 1944 when the farm at Le Haut Bois was bombarded as the Germans retreated under counter-attack. I wanted to see if there'd been swallows in the sky, bees on the roses and to see how big the apples would've been. I wanted to know because I'd found the cold-blooded list of war damages Marcel had claimed from the Ministry for Reconstruction.

Sheet 1 Animaux de Basse Cour, the farmyard. 1 rabbit, *race commune*, year-old meat, stolen by the German Army. 9 hens, *race commune*, 2 years old, stolen by German Army.

Sheet 2 harvest ungathered. Cereals, spring oats, 10 *ares* uncut, mown by Germans. Common barley, uncut, 10 *ares*. Mown by Germans. Tubers, potatoes, variety *abondance de Metz*, 2 *ares*, stolen by Germans.

Sheet 3 farm produce of animal origin. Butter, salted, 20kgs. Crême fraiche, 3 litres. Lard, 5kgs. Honey, gathered 1943, 18kgs, stolen by Germans.

Sheet 4 Bee Keeping. Honey in hives, 25kgs, burnt. Embossed wax, 2kgs 5, burnt.

Sheet 5 Harvest done. Forrage, natural hay, 10

quintaux, 2nd quality, in bulk, stolen by Germans.
Sheet 6 Farm produce vegetable origin. Wheat
straw, harvest 1943, machine baled, 10 *quintaux*,
stolen by Germans. Cider, apple 4°, 400 litres,
stolen by Germans.
Sheet 7 Orchards. 12 cider-apple trees 20 years
open air, good condition, value 300 francs each
in '39, shelled by Americans, recuperated as
firewood 4 *stères*.
Sheet 8 Material and Tools. Various. 2 straw beehives, burnt by Germans. 1 iron wheeled open
cart (1943) stolen by Germans. 1 complete for-
rager 4m loaded, shelled in barricade. 1 black
leather draught-horse harness breech (off carriage
thill), stolen by Germans. 1 hammer, 1 spade, 1
medium pair pliers, 1 pair shears, 1 oak cask 110
litres, 1 cotton waterproof tarpaulin 20m^2 very
good condition. 2 sets of 13 white metal 14 litre
milk pails, all stolen by Germans. 1 iron gate
3m50 × 1m25 and 1500 metres of artificial
brambles (barbed wire), both destroyed by a tank.
Sheet 9 Damage to Land. 10 shell holes 50cm
deep, 2m diameter on ploughed land, clay.

The *expert* investigator from the War Damage
department lived nearby, but it took him five years
to make this first report. He wrote and dated his
observations on 10 November 1950. After having
acquainted himself, he said, *with the declarations in the
claim for compensation in the above nine documents, I
established them compatible with war damage, but to the
exclusion of those claims corresponding with damage tech-*

220

nically attributable to another cause. This was almost the same sentiment as the report I received for the break-in. Same old words too; *sinistre, procès-verbal d'expertise*.

It was the contempt in the investigator's report into my own *sinistre* that turned my retreat into desertion. The ludicrous fuckin self-importance of the verbage: *we transported ourselves to the place, and there, in the presence of the interested party, we proceeded with the operations which had been confided in us. After enlightening ourselves with all the means within our ability, we conclude the following . . .*

Everything was 'so-called' or 'does not seem', a cold disbelief at the non-conformity of my life. The house had offended their sense of the proper, I was living like old Juliette, shitting in the same tin bucket.

They'd examined the house window by window and found it unprotected. They found a discrepency between the number of rooms declared and the actual number, which they found difficult to determine. Everything about the house was referred to as '*le risque*'. Each room was '*what we have called*' and the report qualified itself by saying '*this means that it has an open chimney . . . the meals are prepared here because there is the presence of a gas oven and a woodstove. Therefore they must eat here too. The place we have called the "kitchen" is because it has a water tap. The cramped nature of it allows no one to eat there . . . The attic is partly fixed up as a "bedroom" but with absolutely no means of heating. The floor is rough and the beams are covered in mould where the roof leaks . . .*'

The investigator concluded that one or more

221

unknown individuals broke in without trouble. It said that Joy was not present during the day of their investigations. It said the precise time of the break-in had not been communicated. Up to the day of the report the authors of the crime had not been found.

Damages amount to replacement of two windows 44 francs.
Items not valued by receipts, 13.600,00 francs, present valuation established despite total absence of proof.

I collected the cheque myself, the perfumed broker handing it over like I'd won the transistor in Sainte Catherine's prize draw. The way he said well done, like he knew I'd fooled him.

At first, that final winter, I hadn't understood how Juliette could let the place collapse again after its huge post-war reconstruction. That feat of detachment with her life still inside it, like she'd died in the bombardment but was still out in the fields watching, smelling the flames. Even less so when I found the forms, the claims, the years of paperwork, declarations, investigation, invoices, estimates, the mass of materials, the replacement stock, machinery, the lost time, the moving of stone. But then my life with Juliette had started from the wrong place, her death. She was filth and stench, she was illness and bitterness, she was the unused medicine she'd thrown in the garden, and she was the last colour snaps of a shapeless widow in housecoats and dresses she'd bought off some *bonhomme* who drove round in a

222

van. So when, against those odds, I ceased trying to find love or compassion for her but saw myself at Le Haut Bois becoming her, I drew nearer some truth.

In one photo she's standing outside the cowshed, weeds halfway up the wall, the garage doors locked on Marcel's car. Her hair is thin and grey, her hand, like a root, spans the top of a clay flower pot against her side. The light of a summer afternoon blinds the wall, whitens the cobbles in the yard and bakes the creosote on the garage planks. Someone had sent her this photo, an exposure of her loneliness, a completely useless gesture.

Then I'd stood there myself and had my own photograph taken. A visitor took it, someone I didn't even know, someone else's cousin sent round to lend some cheer on a hot summer afternoon. I'd asked him inside for a drink in the cool shade, but he followed me back outside when I went to fetch some white wine from the fridge in the old cowshed. When I re-emerged he was standing there with his camera, a pocket automatic which he aimed and clicked. For the second picture I raised the capped bottle to my mouth, pretending to drink. He sent me the photos. I'm standing in Juliette Macé's place, the weeds are clambering back up the walls, my long hair is grey, tied back and coming apart. *Joggings* with baggy knees, torn T-shirt.

And then there's one of me standing among my flowers, just like the one of Juliette and her own blooms. Her red-painted clogs are stuffed with carnations and hang off nails from the wall. In hanging pots are dahlias, marigolds and I don't know what else. In their place I'd put onions on the nails to dry and potted herbs along the wall. I've burned one of the clogs, the animals are dead but the one goose mopes by the stagnant *mare*. It's the *quinze aôut*, 15 August. The day death came through the orchards. The war was over. I forgot to count the swallows, watch the bees, admire the apples. But I was free to go now.

TWENTY-TWO

Sunrise. The jingling of Sergeant Wabwire's keys. He unlocked a cupboard and took out his toothpaste, squeezed some on a brush with half its stooks missing then locked the toothpaste up again. He cleaned his teeth and rinsed his face under a standpipe outside. The sun crept over the tin roofs. The sergeant let us drink tea outside and stretch our legs. He looked very smart that morning, cap straight, spare uniform brushed and stiff.

— You have cigarette?

I gave him a Rooster but he didn't like it.

— No Benson? No other one?

— No Benson, I said. When does the fat man come?

— Fat man? Hahaha. No fat man is coming.

— The Chief.

— The Chief is not coming.

— He said nine o'clock.

— Yes. Corporal Gabula will take you.

— Where?

— To Area Chief. Give me another stick.

He tucked it behind his ear. Joy was standing on her own, her back to us.

— Hey you, Miss, the sergeant said. It is safe. These are my orders. You are free. Go away to your lodgings.

225

And Joy shrugged in that way she had and walked off through a gap once blasted in the hedge towards the township. Not a word, not a gesture. Like we'd never spoken to each other before.

— Caw, Wesley said, out by fire exit an' all.

— Out with the empties, I said.

— You like the black girl, gentlemen? the sergeant said. Our Ugandan girls? Kenyan girl?

— Yes, I said. We like everyone. Where is the Area Chief?

— He is here.

— When did he come?

— He is busy.

Wesley was slotting his teeth back in his mouth. When he woke he'd found a seething dome of cockroaches feeding off them on the floor.

— Where's yer *choo* man?

Sergeant Wabwire called Corporal Gabula to show the gentleman the water close-it.

Wesley came back rubbing his hands.

— Right youth, where's this Gabula, he said.

— I am here Mister, Gabula said, standing in the doorway with our passports. He looked at the photos but couldn't put a name to either of us. We can go now. This way.

The sergeant was tidying his desk.

— I shall find the lorry for you, he shouted after us.

We followed Gabula along the verge. A girl with a lump on her face smiled at us through the hospital fence. The English road signs with their black and white hooped poles stuck out from flowering bushes.

226

White fences and mango trees bent laden into the road. Gabula took us through a short cut. Fresh white paint on wooden bollards linked by a grey chain circling a flagpole. The flag twitched, a crested crane of yellow, black and red stripes. We took a side path between concrete sheds full of charcoal, round the back of Military Headquarters. It looked like an old derelict cigarette factory on a Will's Whiff tin. Metal windows with no glass, bombed roof, blistered paint.

— Well, I said. I fancied our chances till now.

— Aye, Wesley said, mebbe it's the bus depot.

Gabula skipped up a flight of metal steps off an old boat, boots going chit-chit-chit, grinding over broken glass and gravel, stepping across clapped-up drawers from filing cabinets and rotten pillows, the feathers ten to the wind. When we caught up with him he was knocking on doors, peering through gaping holes in the wall, finally stepping into a room down the end of a corridor.

— Sit here.

There was only one chair. He put our passports on the secretary's desk, mumbled something to a girl standing at the window and left, chit-chit-chit back down the corridor, down the stairs and across the grass.

— *Jambo* me dooks, Wesley said.

Two ordinary looking girls, both bored and peeling mangoes as they scanned over their work. Through an open door on one side I could see a Chubb safe blown open, bent up and jagged. The room had taken the blast. The ceiling half down, walls blackened, the usual bullet holes. From the other side of the corridor we heard two-fingered typing. A photocopy of Obote's portrait was framed over the secretary's desk. She sucked the mango off four fingers and handed Wesley our passports.

— Hey, *asante asante* . . .

A voice from the room behind her said:

— Come in my friends.

You'd think the whole thing was another hoax or it was a gangland office in a derelict warehouse and we'd come here blindfolded. The Chief of Military Police sat behind a wooden desk beside the remains of a bonfire which had been roughly swept aside by a twig broom. There was a smell of burnt paper and the Chief's heavy scent. Another brass who could shut the desk drawer by taking a deep breath. There was a silver-tipped cane on his desk. No portrait of anyone.

— It is sad, he said. He took my notebook and Wesley's poems from his drawer. It is sad when these men make mistakes.

I didn't know if he meant us, the men I'd written about, or the Acholi who arrested us. He didn't clarify. He waved the notebook in the air.

— I know what this is. I have been here many years. Yes, yes, Gulu is this dirty town, the police are this and that . . . there is a soldier doing this thing . . . I know, you see. I know you English, isn't it.

— Aye Chief, Wesley said. That's hit nail on tip. We don't know no more about Africa than moon knows about Sunday.

— Who are you? the Chief said, holding out the foolscap and taking the passports off him.

228

— Aye, W. H. Scaife, them's my works, fresh off the lathe, I'm the poet sirrah.

He's gonna get us off, I thought. This pit-village idiom'll wear the Chief out with his Up Country Banter.

— Ah yes, very fascinating this book. I study all night long these poetrys. It is very clever, my friend. It is Shakespeare isn't it.

— Aye sirrah, speck o'Shakespeare spit in there nay doubt. Bit o'rooky wood. Bit o'strut and stress upon a winter stage, hey?

Wesley slapped his leg and shook his head and let out another belch of mustard gas. He took a bogroll tube from his bag and prized out a white pill big as a florin. He held it up.

— Caw, muzzle-loaders int they? Any water on site, Chief?

The Chief was beaten, we could see that. Like he was set upon by pickpockets and illusionists at the same time. He called Locky, one of the girls. She came with a pyrex tea cup of water like from a goldfish bowl.

The Chief leaned back in his broken chair, nodding to himself, turning the pages of my notebook, sucking his bottom lip.

— You see, he said, I am going to England in June to train with your police in Scotland Yard. For six months.

He pushed the passports across the table. We picked them up.

— Can I have my notebook?

He laughed, shook his head.

— Haha, you Breetsh, always trying it on. What are you? Vagabond, fucking about the world, eh?

— No, I said. I'm the unlucky explorer.

— Good morning. You are free to go.

The soldiers had moved out, sweeping west. They'd done the killing at night. Innocent villagers accused of feeding rebels. The roads were open and there were lorries coming through. Wesley jumped one to Juba, a big orange Mack from Mombasa which barely stopped to let him on, the mate hoisting him over the tailboard by the scruff of his jacket. The driver looked at me with his shaven head, big scar mounting his crown from the back and running down his face. He thumbed the trailer, keeping slow enough for me to jump. Wesley was shouting: *throw us yer pack, man, hop up* . . . I was hesitating, about going back and finding Joy. She'd been right. I knew who I was now. She didn't need me. More Africa damage. More white lies.

TWENTY-THREE

Me and Joy were sitting in a corner cafe late one winter afternoon drinking tea with skimmed milk. She was in London, and just phoned up out of nothing, maybe four years after Gulu. Wanna meet, Marmite Kid? she said.

Free of Africa she was playful, laughing at passers-by, spilling salt and sugar on the table, saying God I need a hamburger. She said that in London she washed her hair twice a day to make up for twenty years without hot water and real shampoo. She'd let her hair grow long since she'd left Africa.

We were near St Paul's. There was a deluge of rain, people running, smokers in doorways, flooded drains and water looking halfway up the car tyres. We were talking about: *have you ever been in love?* She reckoned it was all chance, like the third person who came round the corner is the one you fell in love with. So we played that game for a while. Third person, second person, first person. Getting soaked for love. Narrowed it down till it was the next woman under thirty-five for me, the next man under thirty-five for her.

The cafe was wedge-shaped, to fit the crook in two streets, an entrance on each pavement. I said I was going to the toilet, made sure she wasn't looking, then slipped out the door and round the corner. There was only one man looking under thirty-five, and he was fifty yards off so I'd beat him to it. I walked round and went up to the window. Joy wasn't there. She'd slipped out the other door and was coming round the opposite corner. That's how we fell in love.

TWENTY-FOUR

The swallows left their nests in the cowshed on 16 August, the day after the battle. They flew south from Le Haut Bois on 4 September. I stayed on, till the cider apples fell when you shook the tree or poked the high branches with long poles I'd found in the barns. Waited, till drunken hornets were late home and frapped the windows after light, till Aunay finally lost his fields at the bailiff's auction and an orange moon rose at midnight and was still there in the window at ten o'clock next morning.

I filled twenty fertilizer bags with apples, six boxes with butternut squash and parsnips, one sack of onions, one sack of potatoes. I tucked the goose under my arm and pulled the door shut. I'd left the unread *L'Orne Combattante* on the table with half a mug of coffee made in Juliette's pot. Juliette's towel drying on the stove rail. Juliette's clock still ticking. The archives bagged and boxed upstairs on the mud floor. I left my bills, our bills. I left our photographs and letters and cheque-book stubs and candle stubs. Our shoes and walking sticks and maps of Northumberland and books on gardening. The bottled gherkins, pickled onions, nasturtium seeds in vinegar from the barrels. LPs, pictures, baskets. Dried flowers, dead roses. My *Dépot de Plainte* against an unknown author, myself. The investigator's report, the war, the deeds, the death certificates and funeral notices. Even my Africa notebooks.

I said goodbye to Juliette, pulled the door shut and locked it all inside, leaving the key in a crack on the steps for the notaire. I put the goose in the van with some clothes, the produce, the fishing rods. Then I went back for the German helmet, put that on and drove up the lane.

TWENTY-FIVE

The Busoga Railway was the first track laid in Uganda in 1906. Sixty-one miles of it from Jinja to Mbugazali. By Independence no urbanisation or development had taken place and its function as a through route ended. The track and fleet wore out, East Africa dismantled its common links and the Catholics moved in, the Mill Hill Fathers turning the cotton route into catechism.

Mbugazali is a derelict port at the railhead, old trading post buildings, dead loading cranes full of snakes, swamp, dust, tin *dukas*, villagers squatting under the shade of *mvule* trees, mending bicycles, smoking raw tobacco leaves rolled in waste paper, chewing sugar cane. The village is separated from the school compound by a barrier manned by an *askari* in old khaki.

The man I've come here to kill is standing in his kitchen doorway as I arrive, thick hands at his side, hands like mole's paws. Father Grimble, tinted spectacles, his dog collar under a cardigan, shabby in his black school trousers, sheened and creasy. Behind his brick shed a boy fans a thin whisp of smoke over the charcoal *jiko*.

There are four large bungalows at fifty-yard intervals beside the track, engulfed by overgrown gardens. Grimble's is at the far end, red tin roof, mango and paw-paw trees collapsing onto the verandah, cracked walls at subsiding angles, patched mesh, window frames which haven't seen a lick of paint since World War One.

Beyond the Nile basin, the sun begins to set leaving an orange purple stain over the low flat hills where smoke rises from village fires. The fishermen drift up and downstream, trolling for Nile perch in their *ngalawa*, dug-out punts. Fish-eagles, crickets, bats and frogs prepare for the oncoming night. This was where they shot the trailer for *The African Queen* with Humphrey Bogart and Katharine Hepburn.

— Welcome to Mbugazali, Mr Tickner. What did you expect, hmmm?

— I didn't expect such a fine view, headmaster.

My 'headmaster' is jovial but pointedly not 'Father'. Grimble raises his brows above the spectacle line. He isn't expecting this from his Marmite Kid. You can see he's angry.

— Well yes, he says, but after thirty-five years a view is commonplace. I tend to notice only what's missing from my cupboards these days. Joseph! Joseph!

He claps his hands and keeps shouting for Joseph till he appears. His shirt is a few grey nylon strips and his bum hangs out from red flared trousers. His feet are bare and the sweat pours off him like melted butter.

— Yes Father.

— The boy shows respect. Joseph, this is Mister Tickner. He has just arrived. You take his luggage to the guest room and prepare supper.

236

Mr Seaton appears and introduces himself as Maths, a short podgy white bloke in round spectacles who sucks his own mouth. Grimble excuses himself, says he's got the small matter of judicial punishments, and that Mr Seaton can remain as locum. Now a white Suzuki jeep covered in red dust pulls up so Grimble waits. A grey-haired, bullet-faced man emerges and looks at Grimble with an irritated frown. Grimble's pointing at the jeep.

— Be good enough to drive me to school, Father Geerts. This is Mr Tickner by the way. His name may ring the church bell, hmmm? No?

Geerts just shrugs. He looks like a bush stiff. The school bursar, a Dutchman in hide boots, khaki, leather skinned. Grimble is pasty and white and stinks. Killing him is going to be easier than I imagined.

— No Duncan, I cannot drive you up. I intend to sit down immediately with a cigar and a drink. I've been driving twelve hours today. Kamuli, Jinja, Tororo and back to Jinja. I'm telling you, there are *no* exercise books, *no* toilet paper, *no* washing soap. There is only chalk and some ink for the Gestetner. We cannot run a school this way. You always walk. What is the matter now, eh? Is your torch not working again?

— No it's not bloody working. I sent Joseph out to check on the *askari* last night. He probably sold the blessed man the batteries and substituted dead ones. I'm fed up with it. You know I can't plug in the charger till it's fixed. And now the chess computer's missing. Did you know that, hmmm Klaas? My other

237

torch is at school and there's no paraffin left in the tank. Didn't you even find any paraffin?

— No I did not. This is not my day for looking for paraffin.

— So now my girls have to do without toilet paper, hmmm?

— You will be late, Duncan. It's almost dark and quite a queue has gathered outside your door.

— Gracious, I must walk then must I Klaas? So be it. I'm late, but I still have a watch.

— Okay Duncan, you shall have your lift. I may as well put some diesel in the tank now. I shan't feel like doing it later.

Seaton takes over and shows me into Grimble's house. The bare concrete floor is lightly swept. Some unvarnished wooden furniture is smoothed by twenty years of sweaty hands. A three-piece suite that lets the rain in and still has the label from Jivani's Trading Stores and Piecegoods Emporium.

— Like Santa's cave in here, Norm. Not what you'd expect is it? Father's no St Francis.

The kitchen is a simple outhouse, concrete blocks, concrete floor. The generator was a gift from Father Geerts's own diocese and is supposed to be for the classrooms, when the power goes off at evening prep. It powers Grimble's video and the twelve computers in his bedroom. The cooker runs off the gas bottles meant for the science lab. Seaton says there wasn't enough gas for the S6 to sit their A Level practical last year.

There's a fridge, toaster, and a cupboard bulging

with photographic equipment for colour processing. Seaton unlocks a cupboard the size of the bedroom where Grimble keeps cartons of instant soup and mashed potato, crates of whisky, two wine barrels, a box of bullets and an ammunition case with live grenades, fishing tackle, silver plate, throwaway razors, two drums of EEC cooking oil, sacks of sugar, a dozen beer-making kits and an outboard motor.

— Duty teacher always knows where the key is in case of emergencies.

Joseph lays the table in the dining room, starched white cloth, silver service, white bone china. Grimble's photographs are hanging on three walls. His hobby, framed by the school carpenter, colour portraits of his senior girls. They're scantily dressed in leopard-skin leotards or green loin cloths with thongs on the tits. His dancing girls, hand picked and groomed from S5 upwards. Senior S6 are 'privileged'.

— All innocent, Seaton says, just school rules, like senior girls mustn't wear knickers under leotards.

— Innocent? I say.

— No, don't be like that, Seaton says. He's probably harmless.

In the living room there's more stuff. The video, TV, screen projector, laptops, solar telescope, CD stuff, mobile telephone gear, stacks of coffee table books on modern dance and photography . . . Well, you just can't move for the stuff. I look at Seaton for some kind of explanation.

— Oh, it amuses him, Norm. He didn't start out with much . . . as you know better than most eh, Marmite Kid?

— He told you about that? I fucking asked him not to.

— You'll get used to him. Bet it's changed from your day hasn't it?

— I don't remember. I only came here once when I was ten.

— Take a look at this then, he says, leading me into the guest room.

It's on the wall. That photo of me, the Marmite Kid aged ten.

— Father fished it out some old tea chest last week, Seaton says. Had to blow some awesome spiders off it. What made you want to come back here then?

— Is this multiple choice?

— Only asking.

— Yeah, same as me.

I was born in this country, but I'm not a Ugandan, it's not my motherland. I always felt like an occupier. I had a mother who screamed at black servants, then wrote poems about them for the readers' page of the local paper. Quaint little rhyming jokes about the social malopropisms of the *kaffirs*. We lived in Jinja, where my father was an armchair missionary, an ecumenical co-ordinator. His great contribution to the poor Christian children of Uganda was to organise the Sunday schools of England to start a Marmite Fund. Boys and girls put their pennies in the velvet bag. At the end of the year they'd buy a big jar of Marmite and send it to Africa. One year the jar went to a little bush school just started by Father Grimble fresh out from Mill Hill, at a time when delegates of the Presbyterian Church of East Africa were calling for a stop to missionaries and money from the West. They wanted to see an East African Church develop itself, free of distortion. But Grimble had me pose for the glory of God.

The photo, above the bed where Grimble expects me to sleep, shows a *Women's Realm* version of a holy boy, standing in a beaten earth compound holding out a big jar of Marmite to sixty pot-bellied Busoga kids. Grimble stands to the side, hands together like a praying mantis. My father, the Reverend Tickner, stiff as a dried fish, is beside him and Joy's father, the Reverand Cudlipp, stands behind me, arms folded like my head was his personal cushion.

It was my job every year, pose with the Marmite for the propaganda photo sent to the lucky Sunday schools. This is all Africa means to me. I was raised by a black nanny and, at fourteen, I quit, gave my parents no choice. They posted me to England to live with an aunt who needed the money. My mother and father stayed in Africa and the last time I saw them was on my eighteenth birthday, a tea room in Bexhill. All that time drifting round East Africa ten years ago was like a dare. I could've bumped into them any minute, but never had. They're dead now, killed by Youthwingers in the last days of Obote and they didn't leave me a penny. They died at the source of the Nile, at the Owen Falls roadblock, because they wouldn't hand over the car. Reverend Cudlipp put a cross at the side of the road.

★   ★   ★

241

I'm at the supper table with the two Fathers. Grimble says grace and the food is mashed potato and dehydrated tomato soup. Grimble is a man who delights in finding sin. He treats people like treasure maps, setting out with Our Lady's compass to dig up that chink of gold, those doubloons of error. I know what I'm up against this time. Once, Grimble's vision for Mbugazali was ambitious and radical. A mix of English public school, progressive co-ed and finishing school. It's run by a cabinet of student ministers who operate a heirarchy of school courts based on medieval systems of justice, policed by 'reeves'. A school where students bow and curtsy, learn to recite Shakespeare, are taught to dance to Western pop music and given lessons in Grimble's dining room in the art of table manners, dinner party protocol, using a knife and fork properly, and drinking beer in a civilised, occasional manner.

I'd got in touch with Wesley after leaving Le Haut Bois. His attempts to get Grimble defrocked had led to nothing but his own dismissal. We thought maybe I could do better. And how could Grimble resist hiring the Marmite Kid? The idea of killing him only came to me when I saw him waiting for me in his doorway two hours ago. I want to shoot him in the head at the Owen Falls roadblock. The Reverend Cudlipp's little cross is universal.

For Grimble, I'm easy pickings tonight, despite Wesley's coaching.

— Mr Tickner, Grimble says, putting his spoon down and pressing his hands together, allow me a professional observation. I detect some regionalism

242

in your diction. I would prefer to employ Oxford men, but I've learnt that one adapts in Africa. Memo: the passing on of regional slang in the classroom is, shall we say, frowned upon in my school. Know also that the vernacular is forbidden among pupils. By vernacular I mean Bantu, African, Swahili. It is all Urdu you know. Should you hear any utterence other than English, it is punishable, Latin aside. I do not like cats and had to shoot Mr Scaife's with my crossbow. I do not encourage monkeys, beards or homosexuals. You will appear on the outfield at 6 a.m. sharp every morning for half an hour's physical exercise. The unfortunate statistic that more senior girls get AIDS than A Levels speaks for itself . . .

You can't see his eyes behind the smoked lenses, but he likes to reveal himself, dropping his specs which dangle on plastic coated wire. His dying scalp snows on his cassock. His thin hair is manky and he scratches his head, buffing it raw. Unfocused eyes bulge with sarcasm like a deaf man shouting. This is a priest who sleeps in his clothes and his snobbery and catches tick fever from Odo, his dog.

— Are you a drinker or a thinker, Mr Tickner?

I've decided in the meantime to fight the man on holy ground, give him nothing to hook his nose into unless it is bait.

— Tee-total, I say.

— Then you won't be too bedevilled man. Dreadful compromises bring inevitable results. Whisky is a month's wages here. Mr Seaton thinks the local beer factory is about to function once more. This is usually of considerable advantage as it placates my staff. What is your vice, then, Mr Tickner?

— Writing poetry, I say deliberately and Grimble falls for it. His snort is like he's rolled his eyes down his throat.

— Your predecessor mentioned something of the same, only he admitted to it like a man deep in his own mire. Wesley Scaife became a roaring drunkard within three months. Hooked on the local gin, at least that's the way it seemed to me. How else to account for the behaviour of a man who fought me tooth and nail, as I suspect you will too, over the rights of Ugandans and the rights of women. Ugandans? Women? This is my school, Mr Tickner. I am responsible for 912 boys and girls between the ages of eleven and twenty. I have for thirty-five years experienced the working of the Ugandan mind. I have been headmaster of Mbugazali College for those thirty-five years. Do you understand me?

— Perfectly, headmaster.

— Good. At the end of Mr Scaife's long service nevertheless, I threw him out. You will be paid in local currency with some staple foodstuffs as supplementary which you may barter. Mr Scaife, I am led to understand, earns £30,000 per annum in Libya today.

I've moved into Wesley's old bungalow. There's nothing to suggest he was ever here. The door was kicked in after Christmas and the furniture sold down the village market. The bursar has given me a broom, a bucket and a new *jiko*. A light bulb, some soap and a cooking pot. I've come with a radio, a storm kettle

244

and a fishing rod. There are nine rooms in this bungalow and from the biggest you can see the old crane. The house echoes and creaks. The school carpenters have knocked up a table and chair and Grimble has reluctantly donated a good foam mattress.

There's one old dresser in a back room, half smashed, a room with a mesh-covered opening into the roof under which the Port Manager must've lain awake at night with his cocked revolver on the nightstand, listening to fuck knows what sleeking dry scaled and deadly over it from room to room. In the dresser drawer I find a laxative tablet, a red bottle of congealed vitamin tablets, four dead batteries leaking acid and some negatives: Wesley with curly hair looking smug outside the National Theatre in Kampala. A woman, climbing out of bed naked, crying, not quick enough to reach the camera and push it away. In some she straddles chairs or lies on the ground like at gunpoint. The last picture shows the Acholi poet Okot p'Bitek drinking himself to death in the Moonlight Bar, Wesley emptying a bottle of liver scourer into his glass. The only other remnant of Wesley's is an old cork shoe on the back verandah floor and a dead bat in the sink. It's a brooding house, another lair of tragedy, a place of death from those Jungle Stories in 1930s schoolboy novels. Wesley'd said it had seemed as good a place as any to discover if he was a crap poet or not.

I've kept one photograph of Juliette. That's here too, propped on the windowsill, beyond which I can see the Nile flattened by rain. Juliette's standing with

Marcel in a wedding group. The war's over, or the Germans are in retreat. The wedding party's outside on a shale yard against a tall fir hedge with a gap three guests wide blasted in it. The house behind is pocked with bullet holes fired through the gap. The guests wear orange-blossom buttonholes that look like five-pointed stars. Two of the women wear silk stockings. It could be summer, even if the sky looks like it came off the back of a dung cart. One woman wears a summer frock with roses, the men wear the same suits for funerals. Juliette's dress might've come from Paris in the last century. It looks velvet, but it's probably home-stitched from an old curtain. She's buttoned up to the neck, broad shouldered, her waist's thick, her eyes heavy. She's thirty-six now. After this she rarely appears in wedding photos.

I switch my gaze from Juliette to the Victoria Nile. I run my finger round the bullet hole in the German helmet and think of Father Grimble. He's kindly let me keep the photo of the Marmite Kid and his three holy victims. It's hanging beside me, so I can tell Wesley that Mbugazali seems as good a place as any to discover if I can kill a priest.

JOYRIDE

DEXTER PETLEY

A novel of dangerous drugs and dangerous driving

Josh's childhood has always been fuelled by the need to escape, from his car-obsessed Dad, his fed-up Mum, and the assortment of crazed neighbours littering his childhood in Sussex. When Josh meets F. at Highgate Ponds years later he knows she is his last chance. They travel to America, but their desperate journey fails to deliver the carp-filled dream continent Josh had imagined. *Joyride*, Dexter Petley's second novel, is a unique and poetic, anarchic tragedy.

'Izaac Walton with attitude and Mogadon. *Joyride* brilliantly captures the bucolic dark side.'   TIBOR FISCHER

'The American dream is deftly filleted of its glamour by a dangerous Englishman. Petley's style is like acid on a plate, biting into whatever it sees and leaving extraordinary linguistic marks.'   DEREK BEAVEN

Fiction
£6.99
1-85702-999-2

Printed in Great Britain
by Amazon